THE ADIRONDACK ADVENTURE

ADVENTURE

A Novel

Richard A. Boehler, Jr.

authorHOUSE®

AuthorHouse™
1663 Liberty Drive
Bloomington, IN 47403
www.authorhouse.com
Phone: 833-262-8899

Published by AuthorHouse 09/14/2022

ISBN: 978-1-6655-7047-3 (sc)
ISBN: 978-1-6655-7046-6 (e)

Print information available on the last page.

CONTENTS

Randy and Ivanka climbed one of the most incredible wonders mother-nature had to offer – a mountain that overlooked the crystal blue "Lake George". And during the four hours of climbing the mountain in this region of North America, they stumbled upon a natural cave. What was in the cave would forever change their lives…

ACKNOWLEDGMENTS

- To friends and family: [learning that there are no friends – just family]. I'm thankful for all the experiences that brought us closer to nature. Through these experiences, a greater understanding and deeper appreciation for the wonders of nature was developed. And this influenced my inner creative thought processes – in a good way.
- To music = [a wonderful way to express the feelings that cannot be described with words. For me, the saxophone and flute described a place and

time – for learning about love].
This area of life will always
be cherished and appreciated.
To "Rock and Roll" musicians,
especially a modern-day poet,
writer, singer – Jon Bon Jovi &
his band [where the intriguing
ability of a song offers the
ability to freeze time/place
of good love…and also a time/
place of love lost]. And this
influenced my inner creative
thought processes – in a
good way.

- To the components of hidden
evil communities, to hidden
evil networks. Thank you for
teaching me. [I learned what
evil was, what evil is, what
evil could be. And this taught
me to appreciate all that
is good in this world]. And
sometimes, good must reveal

the hidden evil in this world – for the sake of humanity…

- To the future – [I look forward to all that can be in this wonderful life. To connect with a true soul-mate, to enjoy all the wonderful values/morality/ ethics in this society (the United States of America)]. To make and share new memories along the way…

- To all the great authors – especially Stephen King, for inspiration and guidance.

CHAPTER 1

It was the first wind ensemble concert of the semester. Randy sat on stage, paused to start playing his saxophone part for "Beethoven music". The stage was bright with ceiling lights that offered a clear presentation of each ensemble section. One section included a percussion area, with drummers. Other sections were large flute and clarinet areas. Randy was seated in the center of the stage, with the saxophone players. As he waited for the conductor to come on stage and start the music, Randy looked out into the crowd. The seating was "stadium style", with a steep incline. This was the design of the University music center. Ivanka waved her hands at Randy and smiled, anxious to listen to the concert…

After the music concert, Randy placed his sax in its case. He had a music room down the hall from center stage. Ivanka met him there. She had used her copy of the music room key that Randy had quickly made for her, when the semester opened. In the music room was a comfy antique looking couch. The couch pillows were soft and easy to fall asleep on. Next to the couch, was a small baby grand piano. Randy and Ivanka often took a break from the University science studies to find solace in music. She played the piano, and Randy enjoyed listening to "her form of art". The music practice room was small, but private – [a perfect place to hide out and continue to build their knowledge base, build their music foundation, take a nap, and always – build their love for one another].

Did you enjoy the music? She smiled and hugged Randy as he entered the room. She replied: "of course", the saxophone is a sexy instrument! As she kissed his neck, followed by nibbling of his ear lobe. Randy returned the love, with "Ivanka's style of earlobe sucking". They relaxed on the couch and just enjoyed the silence. In the hallway, they could hear people walking through to exit the building. They heard conversations about the music that was played in the wind ensemble concert. Eventually, all the people left the building – and it was silent. Ivanka and Randy had a change of clothes in the music room.

They got ready for a late night "rave", on campus. Ivanka smiled and said that "Beethoven" music is wonderful… but that's not "ROCK and ROLL" – holding her hand up and making an aloha hand gesture in the air, followed with the rapid head banging motion of her head. Randy smiled at her – "what a precious zest for life!". She was the smartest, most brilliant lady he ever knew – an ultimate geek, but a geek with fashion style and strong sense for the importance of "ROCK and ROLL"! She undressed and placed a tight black leather skirt on, with dark skin style stockings. Her shirt was white casual, with a cool looking jeans jacket and black scarf. Her soft blond hair flowed as she used her scrunchie to form a sexy looking "pony tail". She was ready to walk with Randy to the rave gathering. Randy put on a pair of blue jeans, with a tight black t-shirt – which covered and showed some of the muscles of his upper chest and biceps. He added a ballcap to his head and they headed to the Rave.

The University students had many social gatherings that Ivanka and Randy tried to attend, when they could fit it in. The studies at University were usually overwhelming and absorbed most of the time/energy. However, it was also important to find some "play time", or risk losing your mind to the academic competition. And that would not be good, because a balance needed to be established – with strategy. With out this type of approach, there was a risk that the student would fall, plummet right out of the University [total crash and burn, i.e., FAILURE]. Although, Randy sometimes wondered if Ivanka really needed a robust strategy for success... she was just so incredibly brilliant. Randy had to work extra hard to digest the complicated curriculum. Being able to survive and excel was good – he was thankful to be able to achieve… but it was rarely "easy", rarely "simple". For him, it required an intense level of focus at times, and dedication – with strategy.

The "rave" was a social gathering that included "battle of the amateur bands". In the smoke-filled room played various styles of music – all "ROCK and ROLL". Some with an "alternative/grunge" style and others with more of a "heavy metallic" style. Randy stood outside the building with Ivanka. She lit a Marlboro cigarette and started to smoke. She wasn't a "chain smoker". In fact, she rarely smoked. It was only when she attended the raves and a bar, that she lit the cigarette. Randy also did not smoke, but on occasions did light up a cigar or shared a cigarette with Ivanka. She had an interesting way of flirting, with the most subtle approach. Ivanka blew small rings of smoke into Randy's face and smiled. He smiled back at her and said "you should really quit those things". She winked at him, then pressed her front body to his body. Following with her free hand, reaching around and grabbing his backside! Ivanka said "you should get looser jeans", [the jeans you have on are too tight, they are turning me on!] they giggled/laughed.

Ivanka and Randy were ready to enter the music booming building! Then Randy noticed something that stopped him in his tracks [it was a gift, being able to sense the irregular beat of the heart, sense the slightest dimming of a soul...]. It was Ivanka's expression toward him. She looked at him without her usual sweet smile. She then spoke so softly... [it was nice, he thought... nice to see her facial expressions, but this was different]. For such a strong and brilliant woman, there was more to her. Randy gazed at her sad expression and thought that she was reaching for something... reaching for "true love". She was reaching for the genuine embrace of the soul...[he also felt that, very deeply]. Ivanka flicked the cigarette into the distant ground and again blew a small smoke ring toward her lover. Randy gently placed his hands on both of her light pink cheeks...then kissed her softly on her upper lip...sucking her lip into his mouth...Randy followed with an incredible, gentle "bear hug". They just stood there, hugging. At that moment, Ivanka felt all that she had been searching for. The love was profound, the love that was exhibited was felt in an instant! The love was absorbed into her soul. Randy and Ivanka then walked into the rave, together…smiling!

She taught Randy so much about life. He was always a simple guy, a guy who just enjoyed nature and a good piece of literature. The adventure of a mission fueled his inner workings…but, what she offered, words could not truly describe. The night was filled with awesome music, a dark smoke-filled room…great amateur bands that just "rocked". She introduced him to the "mosh pit". Randy was more of the "jock", and did not know what a "mosh pit" was. So, there they were in front of the crowd – located just under, in front of the band stage. This area was the place where moshing took place. Randy was more muscular than the average "metal head, dude". He

9

loved the music, he loved Ivanka… and then, the first scrawny looking "dude" approached and smashed into Randy, continuously! This was the MOSH PIT! Of course there was always "murphy's law" [what could go wrong would go wrong]. After a few smashes, one of Randy's old sports injuries was aggravated, and that "pissed him off". Mainly, because a hair line fracture of the spinal column could be extremely painful! Randy was still a good sport about it though. It's just that, when it was his turn to "mosh back", let's say…it was a "TOTAL IMPACT". The other "dudes" went flying across the floor area! Randy felt better. Perhaps it helped reduce the "surge of testosterone" or maybe it was just the smile and laugh that Ivanka displayed after he encountered his first "Mosh"!

They did not stay the whole night. Ivanka enjoyed a party and so did Randy. The truth was that they valued a quiet night together over any party. They were more "family oriented", and looked forward to spending time together on a Friday evening, nursing a baby [if there was a baby to nurse…] drinking some wine and watching a good movie. Of course, the occasional party was valued to, just not as much as the "family life". Randy thought that this kind of philosophy is so rare in many people. Some would have a "problem" with "a family oriented life style". Randy and Ivanka did not care what other people thought… it was their life. It was their love. And that was all that mattered. After returning to Ivanka's dorm room, they showered and snuggled through the night in her bed. Just in silence, and with a peaceful serenity.

The semester's end was approaching and Ivanka was excited to plan a summer get away to the Adirondack mountains, with Randy. First, they needed to complete some intense studies and sit for challenging final exams. The thing about science is that it is always "cumulative". That means it is always building upon previous course concepts, previous principles, etc. All was fair game when they sat for exams... the amount of literature to digest, to learn, to understand was something fierce. Randy and Ivanka were enrolled in a cell signaling class together – a tough biology, higher leveled course. They were studying for the final exam together. The topic was the human cell and the application of virology in this area of science. The human cell is incredible with sophistication! Truly, a dazzling design of perfection. The outer cell layer was important. It consisted of a bilayer of phospholipids… this "protected the human cells" from the outside world! At the microscopic level, a level that could not be seen by the human eye. But so much happened at that level.

The complex process of transcription and translation were continually happening in the human body, as a state of "homeostasis" (balance) was sustained. And this ensured that at the cellular level, that the body maintained a healthy state (homeostasis). Randy and Ivanka both believed in "God". Some people misunderstood scientist type people. They judged, thinking that science people did not believe in "GOD". Well, this was not true. For Randy, the science knowledge was just more fuel to believe in "God". What an incredible, complex design – the human body! The final exam was testing them on the cellular surface, what was happening there.

At the cell's surface, there were "recognition markers", and these markers were important in the transmittance of "signals" in and out of the cell. And as the "signals" went into the human cell, a long process was "activated", resulting in the production of "proteins" [which were everything]. Some cells were special to a certain area of the human body and what signals were being sent there were directing essential processes to maintain "normal human body functions".

The fascinating part of this exam was how the world of virology impacted the human cell. You see, viruses have been around a LONG TIME. Yes, some theorized that the "viruses" were even older than your friendly bacteria, yeast and mold cell. Viruses had the ability to infect bacteria, yeast and mold cells. The viruses varied in the abilities to infect, but all viruses needed the human cell. Because, in the human cell was the "machinery" to produce proteins. For example, the machinery is the cell's nucleus, the cells mitochondria, the cells ribosomes. The virus lacked cellular machinery, but did have one thing though: the genetic information to tap into the human cell and use it! First, the virus needed to "attach" successfully to the human cell. Some viruses had the affinity for human respiratory cells and others didn't. Other viruses attached to the cells of the human GI tract. Whatever the virus was, the genetic information would be introduced into the human cell and distributed. Upon completion of this distribution, the result was a human cell producing "more and more virus particles". Eventually, the human body recognized that there was a problem and mounted an "attack" on the virus infected cells with human helper T4 and T8 cells, among other immunological events. The result in the infected human body was typically fever, malaise, sickness for a period of time… until the body could reestablish balance (homeostasis).

Part of the exam would probe the knowledge base of student understanding of virus origins. And that was also fascinating because these "viruses" [and there were many different types of viruses] had survived (evolution) many years in "natural reservoirs". This meant that a "bird" (for example) could carry the virus and not be sick. It was a symbiotic relationship. It was when the virus mutated [and they often did mutate… because mutation is essentially evolution – with the goal to survive] that a "perfect storm event" could happen.

Innovative technology was another interest that Ivanka and Randy had. And there were many papers written on the "use of viruses" to specifically target human cells that went "rogue" (uncontrolled cell growth, i.e., cancer). They theorized that if a virus had a specific affinity for certain human cell surfaces. Then, if the virus was changed to be "non-lethal", and further modified to attach to an anti-cancer agent… that could theoretically be a good tool to treat oncological cells… The semester ended and Randy threw all his books in a closet. He did not, could not look at another book for at least a few weeks [maybe a little longer]. Ivanka felt the same way. They were in love, they were exhausted from the study sessions and the exams. Packed and ready, Ivanka joined Randy in his Chevy S-10 pick up truck. They were headed up north for the summer, into God's Country – the New York Adirondack Mountains!

The drive from Long Island, up to the Adirondack mountains was refreshing [about a six to eight-hour drive]. It was late evening when they left for the summer trip. The plan was to arrive in "God's country" by the time the sun came up. As Ivanka and Randy reached just north of the Catskills region, they immediately noticed a significant change in the quality of air they breathed. It was cooler and seemed more refreshing with revival of sheer energy, to all of their senses. The scenery was also very kind to their eyes. They weren't used to so much incredible landscapes; a true representation of mother nature's presence on this earth. And as they continued to drive up in the mountains of the northeast region, they gained significant altitude. At first, the altitude change was not that noticeable… and then they came across a group of low flying white puffy clouds. What a cool sight to see and drive into. A rest area was nearby, they stopped for a cup of coffee. As they enjoyed the cool, fresh air in this area of America – they smiled and pointed to the clouds. These clouds were to close, if they reached far enough – they were thinking that it would be possible to actually touch one of them!

The scent of pine trees lingered in the air, and Ivanka pointed to a couple walking dogs. Many people took great joy, with their fury friends, to visit this part of the county. It was a relatively inexpensive escape from the "real world". There were lots of things that people did, and the activities were fun. It's just that the activities were for "unique individuals". The type of people that enjoyed being close to nature. Taking a swim in a fresh water lake, soaking up the natural sun rays on a small local beach, or taking a raft down the Hudson river… yep, relatively inexpensive but worth every moment in time [what one would call "priceless"]. The secret to this mindset was really no secret at all. It was more in the "appreciation of making a memory". To really understand the importance of making that memory, to experiencing those "memories". Because, these experiences always lived on, forever.

Ivanka gazed at Randy sipping his coffee. What are you thinking about? She remarked to Randy: you sometimes go into a deep state of thought, very fascinating to me lover – but, what is it that you are pondering? He smiled at her and said – you are incredibly perceptive! It's certainly your keen inner brilliance. He continued… I was thinking that in the future, if I had a kid or two – I would love to "make many memories" with them in this part of America, in "God's Country"… because, it's important to me and I would hope I would have a positive impact on my kids, to instill in them, this way of thinking …you know, carry on traditions and all that kind of stuff…He sipped his coffee, placed his arm gently around his lover and just enjoyed the next twenty minutes of silence, together. As they drove further north, deeper into the mountains, the car continued to gain significant altitude. And as the car reached greater heights, the surroundings became clearer, fresher and more open – "God's Country". Ivanka and Randy left the Catskill mountain region and crossed over, into the Adirondacks. They noticed many rolling mountains in the distance. But, of course the fact was they were driving in the actual mountains – roadways carved directly through this great land.

Open Adirondack country was beautiful, and they arrived early morning – as the sun was rising. The air was crisp, fresh and the sun shined brightly on the side of each distant mountain side. They drove with windows open and the radio volume at a minimum. This area was so different from where they lived, where they studied. This area was cooler, with brighter sunshine and a significantly different landscape. What a change! Long Island was surrounded by salty Atlantic ocean, many beaches of sand, dunes and a short distance (forty or so miles) to surrounding NY city life. The mountainous area they drove to was a good distance from all of that. Approximately four hundred miles, north from "civilization". There were no salt water oceans. There were many fresh water lakes, small public beaches with trucked in sand. The cabin they were headed toward was located near a natural fresh water lake, "Brant Lake". They had been there last summer, and enjoyed the campground activities. Just being closer to nature was good enough for Ivanka and Randy. In the evenings they would take long walks around the campground. And on the first night, they were immediately reminded of how peaceful the area was. There was no "light pollution". Walking hand in hand they looked up into the night sky and could see an incredible amount of outer space [more stars appeared, planets, shooting stars, traveling satellites, and darkness]. The ample lighting of the Long Island and NYC areas "polluted" the pretty view of the night sky. Perhaps, not everyone took the time to really look into a night sky. Perhaps, not everyone realized that there was so much to see in that night sky. Lights are great, but excessive lights created a polluted sky that covered the real hidden beauty of the heavens.

The night walk was romantic. Ivanka talked about her childhood, she spoke about her love of nature, her curiosity of the mountains. The history of the Indian culture in the Adirondack area and in the United States. The history that she studied in some University coursework. Randy was fascinated with her soft romantic talk, as they walked under the pretty night sky... Randy did not enroll in any historical Indian culture courses at University. But he did take many sociology classes, where he studied "marriage and the family", "south American culture", and basic introductory concepts/ theory with pragmatic applications in the world. He always thought that if he had time he would have "double majored" with the field of sociology. But to balance the requirements of that curriculum with the biological sciences curriculum would have been near "impossible".

As they walked and talked [Randy mostly listened to his brilliant, soft spoken lover] around the campground they noticed a bridge in an area, just outside the entrance to the cabin/tent/RV sites. They left the campground and walked toward the bridge. The bridge was built over a natural flowing fresh water river. And as they approached the structure, they could see shadows hanging from the top portion. What were those shadows? Randy said: "bats", large bats! They were sleeping or maybe just relaxing on this bridge structure. Others were flying in the air around them! The way a bat sailed through the air was so different from a bird. Birds sort of "glided" through the air, gracefully. Bats did not glide so elegantly through the air. No, the bat moved up and down with "flaps" of their wings and then "dropped" quickly, when they needed to. The bat was following a sense of "sonar", where a sound released from the bat, would hit objects in the distance, then come back to the bats senses...a biological "radar" system! Pretty cool, but not good for two University students to get in the way – of a sailing bat, in the night sky! They quickly walked across the bridge, cringing at the site of some of these bats. They were not small bats, they were huge! Randy tickled Ivanka's belly, gently – she laughed. Randy smiled and said: "I think these bats are VAMPIRE BATS!". Ivanka's eyes widened as she giggled...Randy smiled again, then said – just kidding! [I think...maybe they were vampire bats, he did not want to get bit to find out...].

As they left the bridge, Ivanka pointed to a natural flowing water source. It was a well. The mountain water that flowed out of this well was full of "fresh naturally filtered water". They would come back with containers, and fill them with this cool mountain water. The Adirondack mountains were very mysterious. There were large sections of wooded forest... There were hidden caves, some that were tourist attractions and others that remained hidden – untapped by tourists. There were many rivers and fresh water lakes. Ivanka and Randy made their way back to the campground, back to the modest cabin. Inside the cabin, there was a small shower and bathroom area. An area to cook, and a nice sized living room that contained a full-sized bed, with a chair and a couch. No television and no computers. No telephone. They were close to nature. At night, the air was extremely cool – but refreshing. They changed into soft winter pajamas [even though it was summer, the mountains were to cool for summer clothes in the evenings]. Ivanka and Randy crawled into bed, together. They loved each other. And they showed their love with incredible affection and sensuality – often. Randy supposed that some couples had a schedule when to "share affection". That seemed silly to Randy and Ivanka. To be affectionate, to share this kind of connection was an essential area of their relationship...it should be an essential area of any relationship. It was natural for them though. They loved, they loved often. Sometimes they did not share affection...and that was okay... however, the natural attraction [similar to a one magnet coming together with the end of the opposite magnet] they had for each other was there. And they loved that connection of the souls.

Under the warm blanket, Ivanka climbed on top of Randy and shared all the love she could possibly share with him. He did the same with her, connected as one soul and two bodies. Time, length of time was not there... because, as they connected under the warm blanket, time did not exist. They were together at that moment, in another dimension – not of this world, perhaps not of this universe or galaxy. And when they returned from this special place, they snuggled together... falling asleep in total harmony. They woke early, to the sound of birds outside the cabin. It was so peaceful, to wake up with the love of your life – to wake and see the sun shining into the cabin windows. To smell and feel the fresh mountain air entering your lungs. A piece of heaven on earth! Randy cooked breakfast for Ivanka. She was showering and getting ready for their trip to brant lake. They ate together then left for the fresh water lake. At the lake, there was a small beach area. They placed a blanket down and rubbed sun tan lotion on each other's body. It was going to be a nice day at the lake. The scenery was so incredibly wonderful. In the distance, the mountains showed shadows from the shining sun. The rays of sunlight also reflected off of the natural lake water. In the lake was an area roped off, for swimming. Some distance out passed the roped off area was a square wooden dock, floating. It looked to be anchored out there in the lake, since it was not floating anywhere…it was just stationary, remaining in that one area of the water.

As people gathered on the beach, Ivanka and Randy napped in the warm sunshine. After a few hours, Ivanka woke Randy gently with her soft hand. She asked if he knew what was down the road, just next to the beach. Randy smiled and got up. Let's go explore! They walked off the beach and down this narrow, private road. As they walked, the beach disappeared from their site. The road continued to follow the natural lake, and at the end of the road was a dead end. It cleared to a large tree. The tree was deep rooted in the ground and reached diagonal into the fresh water lake. A long rope was hanging from one of the tree's branches. Randy grabbed the rope and readied to swing into the lake! As he left the road, he dangled gracefully from the rope and made his way through the air – quickly. And as he peaked, well into the lake's fresh water – he let go of the rope... and tumbled into the water. As he entered the water, it felt fresh and cool. He went deep into the lake water, reaching the bottom that was full of plants and algae. Randy surfaced and saw Ivanka holding onto the rope. She looked so pretty, with her fashionable plaid red/black bikini and golden long wavy hair. Ivanka grabbed the rope tighter, and traveled quickly into the lake with Randy. Together they swam to an area of the lake where they could stand, waste deep. This area of the lake was private, it was peaceful. The water was cool and fresh. So much different from the time they spent in the salty ocean waters of Long Island. They held each other and kissed. Ivanka talked about her sister planning to marry her boyfriend. Randy smiled and said: "how's that? They just started dating…". She giggled… well, she said that she is planning to marry him… he just doesn't know it yet! She snuggled her wet hair and pretty eyes into Randy's muscular chest. He felt that what she meant to say was not "her sister", no, he thought she was attempting to send him a signal that she wanted to marry him! Randy appreciated her love and just wanted to remain in this place/in this time forever – with the peace of the mountain lake around them; with her long, wet blond hair and pretty eyes nuzzled in between his two pec muscles – close to his heart.

Ivanka and Randy returned to the cabin, later that day. The sun set and the campground quickly turned into a pitch Adirondack style darkness. It was good though, there was no light pollution. The darkness was different than what they were accustomed to. It opened a "new world", to the human senses. The night sky was spectacular in the Adirondack mountains, showing more bright stars than would normally be seen from other southern regions… the Long Island region had too much unnatural light.

Randy started a campfire, just outside the cabin. It was nice.

The wood burned with bright yellow, orange, white and blue flame – representing the various heat intensities. It was the scientist in him! Admiring the colors of a campfire – why did things burn with different noticeable colors? There could be some impurities in what was being burnt...that could be a reason. And the temperature differences, with respect to the length/time of burn also offered a change in what the human eye could see [within the realm of "the visible light spectrum". Anyway, he told himself to simplify and stop with the scientific explanations! It was camping! And that was really all he needed; to feel the heat from a nice campfire – as the cool, dark mountain breeze blew past him]. Ivanka was preparing some treats, inside the cabin when Randy sat down in a lawn chair, too close to the camp fire. The serenity of the campfire, with the nice warm temperature helped him fall immediately asleep… [that and a beer he had chugged helped him fall asleep…] Ivanka came outside with the treats only to be startled. Randy's legs were crossed, with his sandals too close to the campfire!

The bottom of his rubber sandals had become intensely hot; they were smoking! And Ivanka screamed! Randy woke instantly, felt the heat on his feat – jumped to his feet and said "holy shit, my sandals are on fire!" They laughed as he kicked the heated sandals into the cool pine needle filled ground. She smiled, hugged him and asked if he would like to roast some marshmallows? They did, together – followed with the creation of the "smores", an added sweet treat. Chocolate, graham crackers – and melting, oozing hot marshmallows…

they enjoyed the sweet treat. Randy and Ivanka sat by the campfire, enjoyed the company of one another. They drank plenty of alcohol – only to get to a "level of silliness", Followed by the presentation of cool "ghost stories" – which were always fascinating to Randy. That is, to hear the thought process of Ivanka. She had the ability to improvise and entice. To really bring you into one of her stories. And if the story was a "ghost story", near a campfire… with a few beers… That was a perfect storm, which lead to scaring the hell out of him. They kindled the campfire through the night, then eventually went inside the cabin to fall asleep together. It was a nice day and night, with great memories – a good start to the summer in the New York Adirondack mountains.

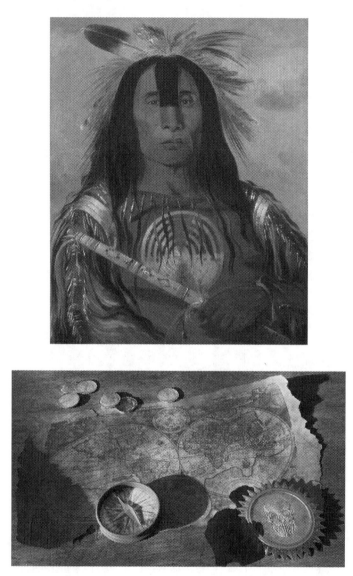

There were Indian tribes in the
New York region. The tribes spanned

the lands of Long Island, New York –
and entered into the Catskills. Just
north of the Catskill mountains was
the Adirondack region, where Randy
and Ivanka were enjoying a romantic
summer getaway – a getaway from
the daily routine. An escape from
the "civilized world" - where they
were constantly challenged to work
through the intense curriculum at
University. It was a good thing to
get closer to nature, even if it
was only a weekend, or an extended
weekend. They were thankful that
they were able to find a way to
spend the summer together, in the
cabin, closer to heavenly clouds
and mother nature.

There was a robust history in
the New York lands. Many Indian
tribes thrived in the Adirondack
mountains. Especially, the "Mohawk
tribe". They knew the land, the
mountains, the forests well – and

these lands held many secrets. There were uncharted areas of the forest that had not been explored by the "average tourist". There were many "hidden" natural caves. These holes in the earth led to uncharted areas, and were fascinating to Ivanka. She had studied many details of the Indian culture at University.

Randy recalled a trip he had taken, out to eastern Long Island. There was an Indian reservation, where most "civilians" were not allowed travel. Randy was working as a medical transport driver, and needed to enter the reservation to pick up an "Indian patient", for transport to a local hospital. As he entered the reservation, he immediately noticed that the land was different. There were no "traditional American" style house numbers and no street names. It was difficult to follow directions on the

Indian reservation. He was quickly lost on the lands, and continued to drive deeper into a forest. The forest opened to a graveyard. And he noticed a sign that had arrows, and bullet holes in it… Not a great place to get lost! He eventually found his way to the pickup house, and transported the patient. Randy was thinking about the "Indian tribes" and his experience on the Long Island reservation.

Ivanka woke and smiled at Randy, who was sitting on the cabin deck – drinking a cup of coffee. He was noticeably lost in thought… thinking about the Indian tribes. Ivanka joined him, with coffee and started talking about their plans to hike up a local Lake George mountain… She wanted to prepare for the day trip. She sipped her coffee and enjoyed the morning with Randy – the fresh mountain air and scenery.

The Indian culture was plentiful – rich in history. The tribes had been in the New York Adirondack mountains for hundreds of years. Maybe even longer… The Indians had a keen sense of nature. They were close to nature, they understood that nature was close to the "after life". A force that was not to be disrespected. They worked the lands, lived off of the land and were one with the mountains. They were also great warriors. The Indian warrior could hunt very well and fight very well. They knew the deep forest logistics, the mighty river elements and the location of hidden mountain caves.

Ivanka's studies at University would prove helpful in this area. Especially as Randy and her traveled up a local mountain. She also had a contact in this area. An Indian travel guide, who was connected to her University studies. She had met him, some time ago – he had visited the University to talk about the Adirondack Indian culture. Ivanka and Randy planned to meet this Indian warrior later in the week, and travel under his guidance – around and up the local Lake George mountain… They were excited to meet with him and to explore the mountain! But, that would be later on in the week. First, they were going to visit a group for "white water rafting" in the Hudson river [Adirondack region, intermediate level rafting trip].

It was a cool morning, in the mountains of Lake George. The air was clean, the sky was blue. As Ivanka and Randy drove to the Hudson river, they could see the rolling green pine trees that covered the distant mountains. They came across a small "mom and pop" bakery, off one of the mountain roads – literally in the middle of nowhere. Inside the bakery was a gourmet selection of freshly baked scones, muffins and fresh bread. They purchased fresh coffee and hot blueberry scones.

Outside the building, they sat at a little table and enjoyed the scenery, enjoyed the fresh pastries, coffee and one another's company. It was going to be a great day, they sensed it! Maybe it was the scones talking… maybe it was their mutual intuition they sensed… this day was going to be amazing, as they would soon be at a stretch of the Hudson river. There, they would board a big yellow raft with seven other people, and sail the intermediate rough waters!

They arrived to the expedition site. There were a group of people waiting for the lead tour guide. A medium sized bus just then turned the corner and parked. The guide was in the bus. On top of the bus were two large inflated yellow rafts. The tour guide, Ricky, greeted the guests and asked for everyone to board the bus. While driving to a stretch of the Hudson, considered "intermediate level", Ivanka and Randy prepared for the adventure. Each guest was given a life vest and helmet to wear, for safe sailing of the large river. The river was flowing particularly fast and rougher than normal on that day. The guests could see the quick, choppy river water. Ivanka said to Randy: "if this is an intermediate level, I would hate to see the expert level!". Four guests in each boat went into the river. Randy and Ivanka were with Ricky, the lead guide. The other group of guests went with the assistant tour guide.

The start of the adventure was certainly not delayed in anyway. As soon as the groups boarded the rafts, they were on their way – rapidly sailing down the rough Hudson river! Randy was given an oar and Ivanka had the other oar.

They sat in the front area of the raft. The other two guests were located behind them. The lead guide was seated in the far back of the raft, with another oar. The might of this river was more than Randy and Ivanka would have imagined, would have theorized. It truly was an amazing creation of mother nature! There were rocks in the distance, extremely choppy waters and "quick drops" along the stretch. The lead guided the direction of the boat and shouted instructions to Randy and Ivanka. Paddle quicker or move toward a certain side of the river bank... It was exciting! Ivanka smiled at Randy and they felt the rush of adrenaline circulate within their circulatory system. It was a good rush though, not a "flight or fight" experience. It was more of a "we are having FUN experience", and they were! Ivanka and Randy were making a "memory", that would live on for all of eternity – in this life, and the next. What a great summer. Who knew that the Hudson river could be so intense! After some rapid drops, and avoidance of sharp rocks protruding from the water's surface – they reached a "quiet area of river".

As they felt their adrenaline levels balance out, the guests of each raft heard the lead guide shout: "time to get out of the raft and swim!" Ivanka giggled and laughed. Good thing they came prepared. That is, Ivanka read the details of "white water rafting", prior to booking the trip. The brochure advised to wear bathing suits and swim shoes. With their swim gear on, and their protective gear (the life vest, minus the helmets for this swim) – they jumped out of the raft and calmly floated in the Hudson. It was peaceful, this stretch of the adventure. And nice, to have the opportunity to really be one with nature. In the distance, at each river side bank – they observed deep forest, with bushes. Ivanka flicked Randy and pointed to some markings on a large tree. It looked like "Indian culture symbols", with arrows pointing deep into the forest. Ivanka had a surprised look on her face. She whispered to Randy: "those markings", they speak of the "eternal-cave". They would certainly come back to this area, together to discover what these tree symbols were... And as they continued to discuss the strange markings, Ricky screamed to "get back into the rafts", the river was getting rough again – very quickly, with drop! They boarded the rafts and completed the white-water raft course. After the trip, they thanked Ricky and then returned to the campground cabin.

Ivanka was so happy. Randy never saw so much smile in a lady before! He was happy because she was smiling... Randy recalled a "wise friend's" quote: "if you can make a lady smile, you are seeing heaven on earth (paraphrased)". Randy smiled and kissed Ivanka on her soft pink cheek. They showered, dried with fresh towels and placed clean clothes on. The night was approaching and they wanted to take a walk to the local "ice cream store". The store was a local favorite: "Stewards". The store was the equivalent to the Long Island "7-11", except it had more – much more. Fresh, hot chili! And fresh ice cream! An enormous selection of ice cream, with each and every topping that would complete the "monster of a sundae"! Ivanka and Randy walked hand in hand along the long stretch of mountain road, outside the campground. The surroundings were refreshing, the cool mountain breeze was out of this world – words cannot accurately describe the feeling. As they walked the mountain road, they gazed at the sparkles from the concrete. Some kind of mystery existed in these roads, a history. Roads like this did not exist on Long Island. It added to the surrounding mystery of the deep enchanted forest. Who really knew what was in this forest? Ivanka talked about the Indian history, the tribes, the closeness to nature. The Indians knew of the magic that existed in the Adirondack forest. The mystery of some creatures that lived within the forest. They arrived at Stewards and ordered "make your own sundae's". Ivanka liked cookie dough ice cream. Randy joked about his simplicity. He liked plain vanilla ice cream, with some marshmallow and whipped cream… that was it – good enough for two lovers.

A good way to end the day. Enjoying the ice cream, in a local Adirondack store. When they returned to the cabin, Ivanka stood in the corner of the room – with an interesting gaze. Randy was curious… She said: "wrestle"? he smiled – Randy knew what that meant… where did this girl get the energy from? He didn't have too much time to ponder that question, when he was attacked quickly by Ivanka's "football-like" tackle! She took him to the ground and they wrestled… and they loved… yeah, that was an even better way to end this wonderful day in the Adirondack's!

The Indian Tour Guide

Ivanka and Randy were excited. After a good night's sleep, together... they woke and readied for a hike up one of the largest Lake George mountains! They drove to the base of the mountain to meet Ivanka's Indian friend... Randy was fascinated with the breadth of Ivanka's knowledge, her wisdom. She always surprised him... As they drove to the mountain, Ivanka explained that a "chief" had visited the University to share tribal knowledge with students. His name was Chief Bear and he was a very powerful, very wise tribal leader – in the Adirondack mountains. She guessed that his age was somewhere in the eighties... but, no one really knew for sure... he looked not a day over fifty. And he was sharp, intelligent with battle hardened spirit. At the base of the mountain was Chief Bear, patiently waiting for Ivanka and Randy. Chief Bear with warm gestures, welcomed Ivanka. Ivanka introduced Randy to her friend, mentor and Indian Chief. Chief Bear commented on their backpacks, asking what they had brought with them. They had protein bars, bottles of water, licorice for snacks and flashlights. Chief Bear took out his tobacco filled pipe, lit it and started smoking. Well then, let's get to it! They began the mountain hike. As they climbed one of the largest Lake George mountains, they observed the deep woods. The trees were of pine origin and oak. The brush was immense and the ground was not steep. They were surprised at the gradual incline, as they made their way forward. Chief Bear advised that as they continued the mountain terrain would change. The gradual incline would most certainly become extremely steep and treacherous at times. So, they stopped to survey the area for "strong walking sticks". These sticks would be important to lean on during the treacherous walk. It would also be pretty handy to lean on, which would help conserve internal energy levels.

About an hour into the hike, they came upon a raging mountain river. The river was large and they needed to find a way to cross it. After walking a bit, they found an area of the river that had protruding stones – they figured that if they were careful enough, they would be able to cross the river at this point. The Indian chief stopped Ivanka and Randy, just prior to crossing the great body of water. He asked them to sit on a nearby log. He joined them, across a short distance – on another piece of tree. Chief Bear started a history lesson. The land was filled with mysterious spirits. Even the local Indian tribe was still fascinated by the magic of this area. A long time ago, there were many wars fought between the French and the Indian tribes. Many wars fought between the white man and the Indian tribes… Much blood was shed in this area. As the time passed, evolutionary mechanisms were found and activated. These "mechanisms" were a way for the Indian tribes to ultimately "survive". The wars were bloody and many souls were lost. The Indians continued to move deep into the wooded areas of the Adirondack forest, and eventually they had changed. They were always close to nature. And nature was close to them. The relationship lead to an evolutionary mechanism for the tribal warriors to changed into "good dwelling beasts". Beasts that were faster than humans. Beasts that were stronger, and that could heal within hours of an inflicted war wound.

These Indian warriors exist today and are in these deep woods, within the Adirondack mountains. They are werewolves! The stories speak of werewolves turning humans into the beast with a bite or a scratch to the human skin. There was also one other way to be changed into this type of beast. And that was to enter a river that a werewolf had crossed/or drank from! So - you see, that is why the chief stopped... to make sure they did not fall in this large river! The Chief, Ivanka and Randy crossed the river, very carefully!Randy believed that "supernatural" things did exist. Things that had no real explanation. The werewolf was one entity that fascinated him. He looked forward to hearing more of the Indian culture. And he did, as they continued the mountain climb. It was the chief and Ivanka who did most of the talking. Randy listened, attentively. If he could take notes, he would have. However, that was not possible while climbing a mountain. The three walked carefully up the mountain. And at times the terrain became steep, treacherous. During those times, they held hands – always moving forward and upward. The mountain trail diminished as they got closer to the top. The land was even more rocky, with cliffs – near the top. At times, Ivanka could see fifty and hundred+ foot drops underneath their steps; just a few inches to the side of where they hiked. It took a good five to six hours to get to the top of this mountain. And at the very top was a clearing so spectacular. There was not much land to walk around on.

The top of the mountain "peaked", had some trees and large boulders. A circle was drawn with chalk at the very top of the mountain. And in the center of the circle was a metal spike – hammered into the land. The idea was to place your foot into the circle, and take a picture. They completed the hike to the very top of the mountain! After the photos were taken, they sat – ate some licorice, drank water and enjoyed the distant view. A view that was outstanding! The mountain view overlooked lake George, distant – clear across the region.

Chief Bear was concerned that it was getting late. They needed to start the walk down the mountain, and that would take time. As they trailed back, Ivanka asked about the meaning of the Indian symbols they had seen while white-water rafting. The Chief Bear stopped and replied: "do you want to do some more exploration?". Ivanka smiled at Randy... of course! The Chief was very familiar with this mountain and knew of a natural cave that was located about half way down the trail. As the group approached the natural cave the sun had set, and it was pitch black – dark. The environment changed. For one thing, it seemed more "mysterious". The flashlights were turned on and they continued to walk toward the cave. In the not to far distance, they heard the howling of a wolf pack. The Chief reminded Ivanka and Randy that the wolves in this area were "good". They were part of the Indian culture, with spiritual powers. Some of these wolves guarded the natural caves. Others lived within the caves. Ivanka asked why a cave needed to be "guarded"? The chief paused and said that there were sacred gifts within some of these caves. These sacred "entities" were of very special origin, from another place/time. The entities needed to be guarded from "evil". We will enter the cave, explore – and I will show you. As they were located just outside a naturally hidden cave, they found themselves surrounded by a pack of wolves. The wolves quickly approached and were greeted by Chief Bear. Ivanka and Randy then observed an unbelievable transformation of the wolf pack lead. He transformed into a human! He welcomed the chief back to the sacred grounds. Ivanka and Randy were also greeted. The chief advised that they were going to explore the cave. He approved of Randy and Ivanka; they were students of his – with curiosity into the Indian culture. Curiosity for the sacred grounds, the caves and what was inside this cave. The wolf pack lead cautioned to be extremely attentive while they explored. The cave was filled with danger, especially to outsiders. He then transformed back into a wolf and returned to his pack. The pack then dispersed into the deep woods.

As they entered the dark cavern, the flash lights helped guide the path. The cave was deep and very dark. There were distant echoes within the far reaches of the cavern. About twenty minutes into the exploration, Randy heard an odd sound from one of the sides of the inner rock structure. He turned and walked toward it. Chief Bear tried to warn him not to go off the path… Ivanka said wait! But it was to late. Randy had left the solid cave ground, only to quickly plummet off a cliff! Ivanka tried to run toward him, to grab him... She could hear his yell as he fell hundreds of feet into a dark abyss!

The End (continued in chapter 2)

THE ADIRONDACK ADVENTURE

Richard A. Boehler, Jr.

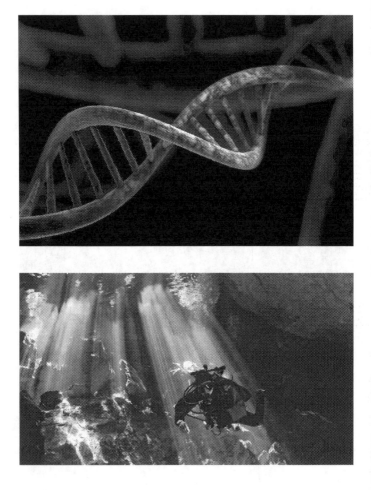

CHAPTER 2

Ivanka shouted down into the dark abyss. Her voice echoed into the distance. She listened… Randy's voice followed up to her: "I'm okay!". She breathed out a sigh of relief. Thank God – he was down there, somewhere… Randy shouted back up: "I think you're gonna want to see this". Chief Bear and Ivanka carefully entered the dark abyss and joined Randy. There was a natural cave stream, lit with a glowing blue-bioluminescence. The stream flowed deeper into the cave. Along the side of the streams entrance were two boats. They boarded the boats, Randy and Ivanka in the first, and Chief in the second.

The water was calm and the cave was dark. In the water, the glow continued and the roof of the cave was high… they used the flashlights to observe, to explore – there were stalactites and stalagmites along the cave. As they sailed deeper into the cave, the water rose and got choppy. Eventually, they reached a point where it dropped about twenty-feet. The boats traveled another half hour, until reaching the cave exit. The brightness of the cave exit was apparent; the water slowed and they guided the boats to the river side.

The three hiked down the mountain and talked about the cave. The chief was familiar with the land, but was mysteriously quiet about the cave exploration. He didn't say much more about the Indian culture or the wolf pack. At the base of the mountain, Ivanka thanked Chief Bear for his time and his wisdom – she greatly appreciated the day with him. Randy followed with a strong hand shake, thanking him for everything. Ivanka and Randy drove back to the cabin.

Ivanka and Randy agreed that there must be more to the cave! And they would return to it, sometime next week – together. They sensed that the Indian chief was hiding something about the contents of the "MYSTERY". Right now, though, it was summer time and these lovers were enjoying the scenery. Ivanka loved nature and she was sharing her personal thoughts with Randy, in the deep woods of the Adirondack mountains. Randy admired her honesty, her maturity, her love… He had been in few relationships with women. But, the relationships were meaningful and not "one-night stands". He was thankful for those times. It helped him understand true love. Most importantly, it helped him differentiate between fake, superficial love and a deep-true relationship. Ivanka had deep qualities that he admired. They had planned to attend a "rodeo" in the mountains, but decided to visit the village instead. The village had a great pizza place where they sat and enjoyed dinner. Through the window they could see the steam ships sailing in Lake George. After dinner they walked together to a local mini-golf place. "Around the World" was the theme.

They grabbed their balls, sticks and started the game. Not competitive, because love was not a competition. Love was patient, love endured, true love exhibited an incredible level of understanding for each person's "circumstances/

history/dreams of present and future". Later that evening, they returned to the campground and started a campfire. As the fire thrived in the concrete pit, Ivanka asked Randy if they could take a romantic walk to the nearby "nautetian well", where natural water flowed through the mountain. The mountain provided a natural way of "filtering" out the impurities. And at the well, a pipe was installed, so water could be collected from the mountain. Randy smiled at Ivanka, and asked her "how did she do that?". Ivanka replied with her cute, soft voice – "do what?" Randy's gaze pierced through to Ivanka's soul – and he said: "be so brilliant, be so strong… and yet appreciate the important things in this life…" [a city girl by DNA, but an immense soul with appreciation for true love, by night]. Randy continued to talk softly, as they walked hand in hand toward the well.

You remind me of the deep honor of a Japanese family. True honor for the relationships within the family. The role and importance of both the mother and father... and the balance with their children, with nature. The United States was the land of the brave, the land of the free. However, Randy's studies in sociology at University and experience led him to conclude some grim circumstances. A fear for the future of the great United States of America. The U.S. lost her way, in some sense. Specifically, a weakness for societies support of the paternal role in family. The father was inadvertently excluded from equations of "predictable success" for his children. In other words, the psychologists concluded and so evolution followed – that the father was not needed for children to succeed in their future lives. This logic was sadly wrong and the ultimate effects of such evolutionary paths would sadly result in a significant weakness in societal foundation. In the Japanese culture, the role of mother and the role of father was full of "Honor" and "Tradition". These elements were being lost in the United States of America, and Randy feared for future generations of American children.

Ivanka smiled with the sun shining in her eyes. She was heaven, heaven on earth. Ivanka knew that in "true love", there was no competition. There was no hate, spitefulness, animosity. She was mature, beyond her earthly years. And Randy's soul felt that connection. Ivanka's soul felt that connection too. She giggled, and remarked — "you are not just the typical scientist, are you?" No, Ivanka said that she thought that Randy had learned/ mastered the art of sociology at University… and she LIKED IT! Her gaze showed the power and intensity of 1000 suns… as Ivanka continued to talk to Randy… "You would make a good husband, lover!" "and even better, deep lover… with a heartfelt connection… I love you! but, you already knew that! Randy stopped her, nuzzled his lips gently into her neck. And softly kissed her, with the beautiful Adirondack mountains behind them. They were happy.

The well was located in a secluded part of a heavily wooded mountain side. Ivanka and Randy located the pipe, right on the mountain. The cool water flowed through the pipe into a tall cement basin structure. They brought one-gallon plastic bottles. The two bottles were filled quickly with the cold water. The place was quiet, too quiet. Almost an unsettling sense of quiet… All around them were thick, heavy brush and trees. Looking into the forest, there was not too much to see. Except for a mountain mist that "hovered", and started moving along the roadway. It was late now, and they quickly got back on the road to return to the campground. The problem was that they did not bring the flash lights!

Walking along the road was becoming difficult as the mist traveled. The road ways in the Adirondack's were not lit with many street lamps… and this made for difficult travel without flash lights or car lights. But even in the misty road, with a flash light – the travel would be difficult. There's something un-describable (not well with words) about a stroll along a dark/misty mountain road – holding hands with the one you love. It's a feeling, a mutual feeling of "togetherness". But more, a feeling of "mutual security". Ivanka and Randy walked with arms together, until they reached the campground. They could see the light from the cabin campfire in the distance… the feeling was "romance", a "heightened level of complete secured love". Strolling along a roadway, with no vision…only the thought of "trust". Trust for one another. After they arrived at the cabin site, Randy moved some of the camp-wood. He then added a few new pieces. Ivanka grabbed two sticks and a bag of marshmallows. They sat in front of the warm, bright fire – with the cool, dark woods surrounding them. As the marshmallows roasted to a light brown crisp, Randy opened two cool-beers. They shared the beers and enjoyed the sweet treat. Ivanka wondered if someone or "something" had been watching them, during their recent stroll back to the campground. Randy laughed, but then displayed a face of seriousness... You know, come to think of it, I did get the feeling that someone/something was watching us. Sort of a "sixth sense" [where a person can actually sense when they are being Watched].

Ivanka thought she heard some howling in the deep forest too. Well, it added to the mystery and the romance of the Adirondack mountains! There certainly was an immense history in the area. The Indian culture, the wars from the past, and the evolution of the Indian tribe to werewolves... Randy believed that there was much more to discover. Ivanka agreed. She planned to re-visit the cave with Randy. She talked over the

crackling campfire wood. Ivanka knew
of a legend, in these parts. It
seemed to be a "stretch of the
imagination". However, since the
start of the summer was already
filled with significant wonders –
she presented the "area legend" to
Randy. The study of Indian culture
at University was full of the
most fascinating stories. One in
particular, relates to our biological
science curriculum! Randy raised an
eye brow, chugged the beer – and
kissed Ivanka on the ear… [which
quickly turned into a gentle suck
of her earlobe…] She chugged her
beer, then started the story.

Deep in an Adirondack cave held a
secret, "control of a telomere". You
recall that we live, that we survive
through a very complex system of
"internal homeostasis mechanisms".
At the center of human balance
[homeostasis to sustain life] is

the control of cellular growth. The cells of the human body, in every area of the body must continually grow. The growth is essential to replenish the cells that have reached their "shelf life". The old cells are broken down, brought to the liver and discarded. The fresh cells continue to replace all the needed cells for normal body function. The problem is [one of the biggest problems with the design of our human life, in Ivanka's humble opinion] that when the cells divided and replaced the old worn out cells (a process called mitosis), the ends of the "cellular blue-prints" were chipped away, they got shorter! Randy listened to brilliant Ivanka. She fascinated him. And he knew that it was not only the buzz of the alcohol [loosing track of the beers…he wondered why having shorter microscopic genetic telomeres in the body was a problem?]. He could listen to her for hours, for days, for years… for a life-time! Randy interrupted in a semi-drunken stoop – So, what you are saying is that when the internal blue print (our chromosomes) runs out of "telomere" length… we are fucked! She laughed… You are drunk!

Well, yes… basically that is it – we only have a certain amount of internal cell divisions before life ends for each and every human being. That is of course, if other diseases don't attack and beat the human body balance first! If the other human diseases don't get you… you will eventually reach the last bit of chromosome telomere length… and no more effective cellular mitosis will occur… then we die. Unless, there was a way to slow the internal human cellular telomere destruction [or protect the length of the genetic material, during and after each division process]. If there was a way to replenish the cellular blueprint, life would be much longer than 80 to 110 years! And, in the Indian culture legend... there did exist a water fountain with the natural ingredients for this [THE SOLUTION TO THE TELOMERE PROBLEM!] Randy smiled at her and asked if they could go into the cabin. She smiled back at him, and enjoyed finishing her cool beer. Ivanka grabbed Randy's arm and carefully brought him into the cabin. She was careful to guide him into the bed... [even a semi buzzed gentleman remained "a gentleman"].

At least, that was Randy... they were in love. She removed her clothes. Randy gently kissed in the center of her chest, between her two breasts... the kisses turned into soft licks. He could feel her hum lightly. His kisses moved up to her chin and lips. It was a good night for Ivanka and Randy... and it ended bare skinned with a connection of the souls, between the sheets.

Return to the Cave

They returned to the cave. Just before leaving for the trip, Ivanka made sure to pack all the essentials in her school bag. She brought flash lights, glow sticks, rope, bottles of water, and protein bars. At the base of the mountain Randy parked the car. Ivanka had one good tool with her, a compass. She was a good navigator. They hiked into the mountain and back to the mouth of the cave, fairly easily. A "beginner" or anyone else would have had great difficulty finding this natural cave. It was hidden well. Not only was it deep in the forest, but it was on a mountain side and hidden naturally with the environment. Inside the cave they started to walk together – with lit flashlights.

Ivanka respected the Indian chief, but she felt that he was hiding something. When Randy and Ivanka reached the area where it "dropped", they remembered that the cave stream exited the cave. It was to simple. It was almost as though the chief wanted them to exit the cave and not explore deeper... so, they continued past the drop off area. Immediately they noticed that the trail became narrow. It started to sink. They continued to explore the inside of the cave. The compass helped Ivanka navigate. The exploration was silent at times, because Ivanka wanted to "listen". She could hear what sounded like running water. Another stream somewhere deep in the mountain cave? The travel in darkness felt peaceful. Randy felt safe with Ivanka and she felt happy, just walking the path together. As Randy walked, his mind opened and he "day dreamed". But, it was more than a dream. More like a place and time... not too long ago... Randy and Ivanka had been good friends for a good amount of time, prior to dating. They enrolled in University studies together. And the classes were similar, due to the shared interest in becoming a doctor. Medical studies were intense. It was a breeze for Ivanka. Randy admired that about her. There was a four-month period of time that Randy had to leave her. He kissed her good bye. They cried. But, he remembered [as he continued to daydream, and walk the cave path] that he held her, spoke softly to her, empathetically to her – clearly sharing his belief that there had been "a divine power" directing him to leave for a scientific experiment. He said: "it's only four months or so", I will be back... I have to go... it's scary, jumping forward into an abyss of darkness/uncharted territory. But, sometimes, it is driven by something or someone greater than oneself. You know... I think it is part of a greater, divine plan [maybe not a good word, more like "manifest destiny"].

They were apart... and four months did seem like four decades – that's the truth. There were no phones... that was not possible in the place he traveled to [deep in a forest, near the Great Lakes]. Mail did get sent though – at least it was something... and it was... imagine receiving "perfume soaked" letters with the lyrics to country love songs? Something that words will never be able to accurately describe... it was just a good way to reach the soul. Randy finished the scientific studies and traveled to the train station. There, he got a fresh hair-cut near the ticket booth. On his way to picking up a train ticket to board the train, he noticed a music store. The store had a great selection of R & B music. He loved the music group "Boy II Men". It was perfect. He bought the "Boys II Men" CD. The two songs he loved were (A) I'll Make Love to You and (B) End of the Road. The group was so talented. But, even more... it was the innovative style of music that Randy loved. Randy brought that music CD back to University. The CD was in his school bag. He was thinking that after they returned from this cave exploration, he would play the CD in the cabin and open a few bottles of red wine with Ivanka… He wanted to surprise her. That was all he longed to do, after being in total isolation for such a long time. He just wanted to share an incredible memory with the lady he loved – a romantic memory, with good innovative soul music; "Boys II Men". He snapped out of his day dream, as Ivanka stopped walking the path. She could see a stream of water flowing up ahead…

The stream was moving quickly and it opened into a larger body of water. Randy found a boat on the side of this river. They boarded the bamboo style boat and proceeded down the river. There was some significant distance, the river started to slow and widen. After a drop of about twenty-five feet, into another path of water... they could see a bright blue luminescence, coming from the water below the boat. It was pretty and mysterious... The space opened up into a large cavern, with an opening at the top. They could see the sun beams shine into the top opening - reflecting onto the inner cave water. It wasn't the sun light that was causing the luminescence in the water, though. There was something else... Ivanka was fascinated in this area. She said to Randy: "you wouldn't think that there was anything magical about this place". It is in the natural Adirondack landscape. No one would ever suspect that a whole culture of Indians evolved to be closer to nature, to thrive deep in the forest as wolves. And no one would think that there was something very important about this specific lake of cave water. She did not know how she knew that. Perhaps, it was a feeling, perhaps, it was more – a sixth sense… Ivanka asked Randy to empty two water bottles, and refill them with this cave water. He did, and then they climbed the cave to escape from the open space, at the cave ceiling.

Ivanka and Randy drove the mountain road, slowly, heading back to the campground. The slow drive was intentional. It was to enjoy the scenery, to enjoy the fresh mountain air flow into the open truck windows. They noticed clouds in the air, that were so close to the truck. So close, that they could almost reach out and touch these clouds. It was truly amazing… the landscape, the area was beautiful. They were instantly reminded of their altitude, being high in the Adirondack mountain. This meant they were closer to the clouds, closer to the heavens! Ivanka entered the cabin with Randy, just as the mountain sky opened. They could hear the drops of rain falling outside, on the cabin roof. They could smell the ozone in the air, just prior to the sky opening... it lingered shortly as the storm started. These storms were different than the typical Long Island storms. The rain in the mountains could be fierce, the thunder crackling loud and the lightning bolts... the strikes did not have far to travel. From the corner of his eye, Randy was surprised as a bolt of lightning struck a tree, right outside the cabin! Ivanka's jaw opened, in awe of the heavenly sight. She asked if Randy would start an indoor fire, with the wood next to the fireplace.

He smiled, turned on music [very low volume] and started the fire. Ivanka popped open a bottle of red wine – she read his mind. The night was peaceful, even though a mountain storm raged outside the cabin. They snuggled on the couch together, sipping red wine and listening to a new CD "Boys II Men". Ivanka liked the music. Randy was happy that they shared a mutual appreciation for the "pop-R and B style" music genre. There was something about being in the cabin with Ivanka, protected from a fierce rain storm outside. A fierce storm, but a delightful warm cabin. They rested, gently in each other's embrace – eventually attempting to fall asleep. Randy was wondering what was so special about the two bottles of cave water, collected earlier that day.

Their relationship reached another level – that was possible to achieve with true love. This was an "unspoken level". In terms of science, of nature – their bond was changed from a weak "single bond" to a much stronger "triple bond". And although they did not speak of that bond, they were well aware of it – they sensed it. It was a stronger feeling than the very strong pheromones shared between these two hearts. Randy had longed for affection and sensuality, simply – the caring warm kiss of a lady. Ivanka felt the same way – with all the brilliance of her mind, it was really not that complicated... she longed for true love... and found a way to connect with Randy... she found a way to bring the relationship to another level. This became evident in the night, while she snuggled next to Randy in her soft cottony pajamas. Her hair was silky straight and long. Her skin had a wonderful vanilla aroma. The heat from her gentle, soft pink lips reached Randy's skin, to kiss him good night. She continued to softly kiss him, everywhere she possibly could kiss his skin... He returned each kiss to her, more gently, with more passion. They fell asleep, in each other's embrace.

The morning came too fast. Randy woke first, and enjoyed the early fresh mountain air. The climate was cool, and usually had a moist element to it. Being in the mountains was so different from Long Island. The sounds of nature all around, the fresh air, the view of beautiful pine trees. No light pollution. He was straightening things up around the front of the cabin. Then started chopping some wood logs for a near future campfire. They had plenty of sweet treats. Marshmallows for roasting, graham crackers and chocolate to make smores. The sun beams made their way through the tree branches of the campground. It was a very pretty site to see, especially early in the morning. Ivanka woke to the light sound of music playing outside the cabin. She observed Randy chopping wood, and she smiled. While Randy finished some basic chores outside the cabin, Ivanka showered. After she dressed, she started a fresh pot of coffee – and joined Randy. They enjoyed a peaceful mountain morning, drinking coffee in lawn chairs. Randy was really enjoying the summer. The environment is not for everyone. Some people don't enjoy this type of environment. It's a simple environment, with many mysterious complexities. Randy had always been fascinated with the natural lands. The Adirondack mountains was certainly a keen example of "natural land". He picked up a medium sized stick and started carving the very end of it. The carving of this stick was unique to this environment. A simple way to pass time, a simple way to make a memory.

The end of the stick was carved into a sharp conical point. He continued to carve the shaft of the stick with various patterns. Then he presented it to Ivanka. She giggled as she saw that he had carved their initials in the wooden shaft. He said that she could use it for marshmallow roasting, or she could just keep it as a "good memory". That day, they drove the mountain roads to explore. The roads were cut right through different places in the mountain. Sometimes the roads were windy, and other times there were deep declines and steep inclines. Eventually, they made their way to the main village of Lake George. A tourist attraction to people from Canada, and people from all over the world. There were small bars with live music on the lake waterfront. Boats could be rented to explore the large Lake George. And in the center of the village was a horror museum: "Frankenstein's museum". A favorite of Randy and Ivanka. The wax figures in the house of Frankenstein, included many Edgar Allen Poe themes! And many sci-fi horror themes! They entered the museum, and walked hand in hand – through the dark corridors. As they walked through the narrow halls, they stopped at each "exhibit of horror". The werewolf exhibit was fascinating.

At the wolf exhibit, Ivanka noticed something interesting. Behind the wolf was a wax man. He was holding a glowing bottle of water. She still had the two cave water bottles in her back pack. There was a curiosity that was fueled in that moment. She wondered what in the world the water was? Did it change a human being into a werewolf? Randy shrugged and moved forward to the next exhibit. After they left the museum, Ivanka grabbed some ice cream for herself and Randy. They sat on a bench, overlooking the beautiful lake. The water was in the backpack, and Ivanka wanted to drink it!

The two bottles were full of the cave water. Randy grabbed one of the bottles, held it up to the sun – and observed it. The water was clear, with a light blue "glow". Ivanka was curious. She wondered what caused the glow of the water. Randy spoke about "bioluminescence". It seems that this water is showing similar properties to the "bioluminescence reaction". We see it in the lightning bug. A soft yellow-green glow, in the night sky. This bug has an enzyme "luciferin-luciferase" that combines with "energy". The result is a light flash. The lightning bug is not the only creature to exhibit this... There are many other creatures that show bioluminescence. There are glowing fish, glowing beetles... and more deep-sea creatures. What was curious to Randy was the amount of ATP, the amount that must have been present in the cave water. For example, we could go to a store to buy an energy drink to "recharge" our body. The energy drink is full of all sorts of stuff [caffeine, amino-acids, protein, vitamins, nutrients]. However, at the end of the day – what it really comes down to is the "amount of ATP" that is being generated in our bodies. The "ATP" is adenosine tri-phosphate, which is basically an energy molecule [when the third phosphate bond is broken, a huge amount of energy is released into the human body, essentially]. The more energy molecules you have, the more "energetic" you feel. This water must have a lot of ATP molecules in it, because the glow is steady and continuous – it stays, doesn't diminish in the intensity. Ivanka smiled, and listened with curious ears. Fascinating stuff! Nature really is fascinating! It's our cells… within our body cells are cell organelles. The mitochondria is one of those important organelles, with the responsibility to generate ATP. Exercising, in theory, generates fresher cells, and increases the amounts of mitochondria. A "larger amount of this organelle", will increase the amount of internal ATP… and a person will feel better, have much more energy! What Randy was wondering… was the cave water a source of energy? If they drank the water, what would it do to them? Would they feel stronger, have more energy? In theory, they would. But, perhaps there was more to this cave water than they even knew or hypothesized... Ivanka needed to bring the water back to the University lab. And that was their plan. They would enjoy the rest of the summer in the Adirondacks together... In late August, they would return to Stony Brook University, get situated... then investigate this cave water.

The summer time went by way too fast. Time flies when you are having fun... And they were enjoying each other's company. They were making memories, enjoying the fresh mountain air – the cool Adirondack nights around a campfire. There was sort of a routine that was followed each day. In no particular order, with no firm schedule – but a routine for the things they loved to do. A few times each week, Randy would drive to the fresh water lake with Ivanka. They soaked up the sun rays, and brought tubes to float on for hours in the mountain lake water. On weekends, they visited the Lake George Village. Stopped off in the arcades to play some video games… but, really enjoyed the shooting gallery – where laser guided guns were used to shoot at various targets. The targets were attached to different actions. One favorite was a piano man that would start playing the piano tune, right-after the bull's eye was hit with the laser. Ivanka liked the targets near a water fall. Some of the targets would ring a bell. And other targets would move a can through a wooded area. Long walks in the evening to the well, and lots of relaxation – listening to music, drinking red wine or beer…

followed by conversations around the campfire...

It was August of that summer, and one last trip was planned. They drove north of Lake George, about an hour. As they drove, each mile brought them closer to the Canadian border. They were not going to the border, but did want to visit a place called "Ausible Chasm". It was a natural reservoir, with trails that led into caves. The trails were also cut into the sides of mountains, overlooking the deep raging river below. A boat ride through the rough waters typically ended the tour at this place.

It was early morning, and Ivanka packed all the essentials in her backpack. The supplies included flash lights, protein bars, some rope and the two bottles of cave water. The chasm was amazing. The trail offered a spectacular view of mother nature.

Located hundreds of feet above the raging river were trails to walk. The paths were literally cut into the mountain sides. The only thing stopping the hikers from falling from the narrow paths, was one thin chain. They proceeded through the paths very cautiously. Located some distance on the path, Randy moved ahead of Ivanka. He wanted to get a better view to take a photo... and as he climbed higher on the trail, he inadvertently tripped on some rocks – which propelled him over the thin chain! Ivanka screamed at what had just happened, watching in horror as he violently crashed hundreds of feet below her. Randy lost balance, smashing into the side of the sharp mountain rocks – as he plummeted downward. Each sharp rock pierced his flesh, opening the skin and exposing fresh human bones. The worst part of the fall were the snaps the bones made. At the bottom of the mountainside, lay Randy – broken and silent. Ivanka screamed his name, with no response from Randy. Ivanka quickly and carefully made her way to Randy. He was breathing, semi-conscious. She felted panicked and sick at the sight. And in that moment, she knew that there really was only one thing she could do… She knelt down, beside Randy and opened her backpack. The glowing bioluminescent water was carefully transferred into Randy's mouth. She also dripped some of the water onto his wounds… and waited. Immediately and miraculously – the wounds healed before her eyes, and Randy gained consciousness. It was amazing! He asked for a few more sips of the water. There was something in this water, and not only did it heal wounds, but it transformed the human body…

They drove back to the cabin and began packing for the return back to the University. Before heading back to Long Island, they filled a few gallon bottles with the secret natural cave water. Randy rested in the passenger seat while Ivanka drove most of the way home. He was napping, but felt stronger. He felt younger and different. He felt younger, more alive with extreme energy... It was because of the water!

Stony Brook University

It was the start of another semester together. A full schedule was typically: 15 credits, four classes. The science majors had it tough. Lectures had labs attached to the curriculum. And the labs were long, ranging from three to four-hour sessions, twice per week. That was a commitment, requiring a big block of time out of a weekly schedule. You see, it was not just the time in class. It was really the time out of class that was super challenging [in addition to the in-class challenges]. Outside of class required a level of focus… where they coordinated "study sessions": met friends for "study group sessions", or just [most of the time] spent tedious hours upon hours alone in the library stacks, surrounded by shelves of books. Seated at a desk, reading – highlighting words, re-writing class notes… coming up with short hand words and ways to memorize – concepts/processes/facts/theories, etc. Applying that information was also a great challenge… applying the knowledge during testing was essential to showing the professors that the student not only knew the information…but, it also showed application of the knowledge, which was a key indicator for "understanding" complex processes.

It wasn't for the faint of heart. It required discipline, an inner "want", and inner "need" to learn. In fact, the population of students dwindled by semester's end. Many just "gave up". Others flunked out. And others transferred to other schools. Ivanka and Randy were excelling nicely, through the semester. Part of the success was just due to

Ivanka's brilliance. For Randy, part of Randy's success was just due to his inner desire for discipline/ acceleration for achievement. More of the success, though, was that they were achieving "together", finding ways to meet every difficult challenge "together". It was autumn and the tree leaves were changing colors – to a bright yellow, orange and red. It was pretty! They enjoyed their surroundings. Even though the weeks were full of challenges, they made time at night. Randy usually slept overnight in Ivanka's dorm room. Mid-week, they shared an early class – Sociology [Marriage in the Family]. It was early, very early – 7 AM. That meant they needed to rise super early [5 AM to 6 AM] to get ready. Most of the time, Ivanka woke first to get ready for class. Randy woke second and just rolled over, jumped in the shower – placed a ball cap on his head, followed with clothes… and he then was ready to go. Ivanka spent time straightening her long blond hair… to a silky soft style… and other stuff. Across campus, they arrived at the lecture hall. Ivanka would get Randy a seat in the lecture hall, usually toward the front of the stage [but not that close]. Randy had his routine. He stopped by the University bakery. Fresh blueberry, raspberry and chocolate scones were baked each morning. And he would get two scones, with coffee. He brought breakfast to Ivanka, and they ate together as they listened to the professor's wisdom.

It wasn't all science. The first two years of University curriculum was designed to explore various areas of study. Randy took a liking to sociology. Specifically, the studies of South America. Ivanka took a liking to music and astronomy. Randy enrolled in an astronomy class, with her one semester. It was fascinating, but extremely difficult. It wasn't like the star trek series. No, it was more of knowledge about the temperatures on each planet in our solar system. The pressure of each planet, the type of atmospheres, the land [if land existed on the planet…] very difficult… to this day, Randy was proud to have received an "A" in this space course. He found the exams to be extremely challenging. Like Ivanka, he studied and put in the library hours… and the "A" was well deserved.

The campus was tremendous. And the landscape was full of trees, more like a campus in the middle of a forest. This was good. The forest had many bike paths. To get from one building to the next, you could walk it or ride a mountain bike. Ivanka and Randy did both. Deep in the forest was a marine science building with a laboratory. Ivanka spent time studying marine biology, conducting experiments. That is where she brought and stored the "bioluminescence cave water". They were studying the chemical composition of the cave water. It was fascinating. There were the usual properties: two hydrogen elements and an oxygen central to the molecule. The bonding of the H_2O was the way it should be. What was different about the water was the presence of an odd-looking organelle. Under the microscope and with other laboratory techniques, Ivanka was able to photograph what looked like a "mitochondria". This cellular component was responsible for generating large amounts of energy in the human body. In fact, more mitochondria in the body, meant more energy. There were also differences in the appearance of this cellular mechanism. Ivanka thought that the energy being generated in the cave water had evolved to a "higher output". A level of energy that was more "concentrated". And with a greater amount of concentration in the energy, the result would be an incredible surge of strength; with massive capacity to accomplish wonderful things…

The moon would be in the "full phase" soon. Randy sensed a change to his surroundings. First, he was hungry for red meat. He had urges or cravings for red meat in the past, but this was noticeably different. It was a cascade of an inner sense of "starvation". He was "starved" for red meat. Even though he really wasn't that hungry… this feeling was animal-like. He needed the red, raw meat – and he needed it soon. He would get it, attack for it, hunt for it… kill for it…

His skin felt thicker, rougher to the touch. His nails and hair felt "thicker", with strength. He felt the urge to cycle, to jog – even though it was late in the day, and he would typically walk to the dorms. The bicycle did not appeal to him. He wanted to run, he craved the run, he felt an inner desire to "hunt". To hunt flesh. As he jogged deep in the University woods, he sensed a wild rabbit running through the brush. Within a flash of a second, Randy caught up to the wild rabbit and clawed into its flesh with what appeared to be large sharp nails. He quenched his craving for red meat as he abruptly ate the rabbit. His appetite for flesh was then balanced, for now…

Ivanka and Randy slept in, late the next morning. They had scheduled their course load to allow for one late morning, each week. It was a good thing... it helped keep some sort of balance, to keep a sanity – in a world that was constantly challenging them. It wasn't only the classes. It was everything that went along with academic studies at a University. The atmosphere was filled with a fierce level of challenge. As they walked around campus, the atmosphere had filled their lungs and challenged every cell of their bodies. It was okay though, because with every success came a strong sense of accomplishment. Something that offered a strong inner foundation. And they would bring this with them, as they moved from the present life – into a future life, together. It wasn't just the successes... it was more than that. It was the failures that also strengthened their core. The tests were countless, and always were sandwiched with other course tests. A mosh posh of fierce tests, overlapping each other. It almost seemed impossible to prepare for. How can one study and prepare for a calculus mathematics exam and a physics exam, all given during the same week? And that was a simple example. There were many times when three tests or even four tests were given during the same week. The struggle was there and every student felt it. After an exam, Randy would look at the grades list. Part of the student's social security was listed, on paper next to the number grade. Top grades in the toughest course were typically in the 40s to 50s… and with the calculated statistical curve – an "A" would be assigned to a certain number grade. In some exams, an "A" could theoretically be a "25". Lots of academic failure. Moving past one tough exam into the next section of testing would always include previous course work [so, if you struggled with early semester topics – you would struggle the rest of the way, until it was understood]. So, as the semester continued – all the information learned [or failed to be learned] typically followed into the future exams... there were no short cuts. Failure was built into the curriculum and it followed you, until enough time in "late study nights" met the demand.

Ivanka and Randy enjoyed the one late morning, during the week – together. Academic life was not all intense nerdy studies. A school bus system followed a schedule throughout the day, into the evening. Randy and Ivanka loved to catch a bus ride, off campus, to

the local mall. In the mall area
there was a movie theater – where
they could catch a good movie.
That late morning was particularly
nice. It was a crisp, cool autumn
morning. The University was full of
energy. Randy could hear students
walking outside, in the dorm halls.
These students were heading to
their early morning classes. Randy
smiled, and stretched. He carefully
got out of bed, making sure he was
gentle enough not to wake Ivanka.
A quick shower with Irish Spring
soap refreshed his senses. A shave,
followed by the quick formulation
of coffee was a good start to the
day! As the coffee brewed, Randy
sat in a chair – admiring Ivanka's
soft skin, pink lips, and shiny
blond hair. She slept so peacefully.
He wondered what she was dreaming
about. Probably not too much science
stuff... she probably was lost in a

world of nature, as she loved the Adirondack mountains…

This would be a "light day" for academic classes. No complicated, labor intensive laboratories. No long lectures…it would be a day to either "catch up on some studies" [which was not a bad idea] or to relax a bit and enjoy some romance. Enjoy the time of year, a walk through the woods or a trip to the local mall. As Ivanka woke, she was greeted with a hot cup of coffee. She smiled and thanked Randy. It was nice to be together this morning. They agreed to take a trip to the mall, shop for some clothes and follow that with a good movie.

After the trip off campus, they were "refreshed" and ready to attend another round of classes. In the evening, Ivanka met Randy in a private restaurant – on campus. There were many places to meet, to grab a bite to eat, or to just get a good cup of coffee. Ivanka knew all of the great places to meet. Where the crowds were not found. And that was nice, when you just wanted to catch a breath – and catch up on some conversation. There was a building called the "union". It was one of the campus structures that had been built when the campus opened one hundred years earlier. On the second floor of this "union", in the back of the structure was a nice place to sit. It was dimly lit, and it had one small restaurant style setting, called: "Papa John's Pizza". A simple place. They grabbed two personal pan pizzas, some coca cola, and sat in a corner booth. Ivanka was excited to talk about a finding for the "cave water". She had been studying the water chemistry, on her spare time [where it was possible]. Specifically, what she presented to Randy was the chemical components. He wondered how she achieved this new found "understanding". She smiled and said: "gel electrophoresis"! Of course! This was a lab test to "separate" out the "invisible" components of the water. Basically, a gel was used and an electrical current was passed through the solution/ gel, after placing the cave water in it. As the electrical current flowed through the solution, the components of the water traveled, at different rates – depending on the size of each respective water part. Ivanka was able to get a better Understanding of what was actually in the water!

She was amazing, a super geek, with personality. The pizza was good, fresh and Randy enjoyed the time together. He asked if they could get away from the science for a-while? she giggled, of course! What's on your mind? I think that cave water changed me! I've been noticing a thirst for blood! She thought that he was joking! He wasn't joking around. Randy continued: I find myself craving red meat, flesh. In fact, I went after a rabbit the other night. And it had quenched histhirst, briefly. Randy felt stronger and more energetic. There were side effects though. There were dreams or "visions", since he changed.

He always found himself leaving the campus when the moon was full. Ivanka asked where he was going to, when he left the campus in the middle of the night. That's the strange part about it. I changed into something different, with the light of the full moon. And in the visions, I am propelled to towns around the University. Randy searched or more like, had a strong affinity, for "EVIL". And when he found it, he would shred it apart to quench his thirst for blood! Ivanka grabbed his hand and said: "Ivanka believed him!". She had found other things in the cave water analysis… and Randy's talk completed some of the puzzling questions… [she had, while researching the cave water elements].

Randy thanked Ivanka for her support. He spoke more about his appetite for "iron", a craving for red meat! She laughed and said: I like cheeseburgers, just like the next person. He smiled, and said that it was not like that. The feeling was an inner bon fire of energy that needed to be cooled by the "hunt". A hunt that was part of the craving. And during the "hunt", an incredible aggressive motion of "fight or flight". This was "fight", where the "targeted evil" was ripped to shreds, and eaten! He held his temple with two fingers and softly continued… a long time ago, I was aware of two blessings… [or curses – depending on the way a person perceived it]… the first was the wonderful ability to connect to the heart/soul of a lady. Only one part of the equation though [the lady's heart/soul was the other part of the equation, where she would need to offer her connection to him]… I always prayed and was grateful for this ability to whole heartedly be loyal, content in love – complete, pure happiness. This is a gift from the heavens for us on earth. Not all people on this earth share this gift… but many do, and it is truly the most powerful gift given to humans [and many animals too]. Ivanka smiled and asked why he felt it could be perceived as a "curse".

He smiled back and simply said: "to wear a heart on your sleeve, sometimes results in unintentional heartbreak". She had been in a relationship, prior to Randy, and she hugged him with complete understanding. Complete empathy. Randy was incredibly thankful for this mutual understanding.

What is the second "gift"? Ivanka was curious. Randy continued: The second gift can also be perceived as a "curse", because with it comes great danger. For as long as I could remember, my soul has had an "affinity" to "evil". Much the same way that a positive magnet comes together with a negatively charged magnet. However, the result is something fierce. The mission [with an inner compass from the soul] has always been to "destroy the evil on earth". And with this change, after taking in all that cave water, I have been ramped up to a whole new level of "fight". And the cool/ interesting thing is… "I like it"!

They went back to the dorm room to get a good night's sleep. Randy was happy to sleep in Ivanka's room, since some strange people had moved next to his dorm room. He believed that these "strange" people were waiting till other people fell asleep… then would start SMASHING walls and doors next door – waking everyone up! So sad. Randy couldn't understand why people would be that way… to intentionally SMASH walls and doors to intentionally not allow their neighbors to get a good night's sleep. Ivanka smiled. She heard of that. Ivanka had a friend in the University administration. The University was in-process of removing these people, from their place of residence. She thought, they would probably lose their

position at University, as well. But
that was just a hunch. Randy asked
if she heard about these peoples
names? She laughed, you are nosy!
I heard one name: Leanord.

Back to the lab was important to
completing the analysis of the cave
water. Ivanka wanted to run some
additional tests. She had isolated
some of the chemical components.
What she was now interested in was
the "reactions" that took place.
She was adding reagents to various
solutions, and waiting for color
indicated responses. These reactions
would give insight into the capacity
of these magical ingredients. Randy
visited Ivanka in the marine science
laboratory. The water was clear
in appearance. A blue glow shined
from the 1-gallon container. After
completing various lab tests of the
water, it was obvious to Ivanka that
the properties of this water were

unique. She wanted to taste the water, but Randy cautioned her. He reminded her of his change, especially during a full moon. She continued with her analysis of the water. The properties were fascinating. When applied to the human chromosome, the water was able to "protect" the end of the genetic material. This was fascinating because in a human life span, there was only a finite number of "cell divisions". Each cell division resulted in the shortening of the end of this genetic blue-print. Essentially, it was a trade-off. The constant cellular divisions were necessary to maintain a fresh supply of human cells, that fueled all biological processes. However, after each replenishment of fresh cells, the available genetic material was "removed", shortening the length… this area of genetic material was termed: "the telomere".

Ivanka applied the cave water to the genetic material, and immediately discovered the rapid affinity of its components to the genetic telomere region. It offered "protection", where cell divisions continued, without the shortening of its length!Ivanka insisted that she try the water, and that is exactly what she did. She drank the cool cave water – right in front of Randy! She immediately felt healthier, stronger. The water was life. A supply of life. Randy smiled and asked if they could call it a night. They did, and returned to the dorm room. The Adirondack mountains held so much beauty. Randy admired that Ivanka shared the appreciation of this nature. They stayed up late, talking. They would continue to visit the Adirondacks each summer, camping. They would continue to enjoy the camping trips, and the campfires. And each summer they would replenish their supply of cave water. And perhaps, if they were theorizing all this correctly… they would manage to live a very long, healthy life of love, together. And what they meant by long was 200 plus years!

The season changed from the crisp, cool autumn to a colder winter. Snow fell and they continued their studies at the University. This time of year was truly amazing. It was full of so much happiness, celebrations and appreciation for the holidays [Thanksgiving, Christmas]. They finished the semester, and visited some family for the holidays. During the winter vacation [session], they drove to different parts of Long Island, and enjoyed the natural landscape. The beaches were nice to visit. There were many local parks too. In fact, one large park was a favorite of theirs to visit. It was filled with large pine trees and also a mystery! The stories were not as fascinating as the Indian culture that Ivanka studied at University. But, there were some odd stories that they explored. Ivanka heard a story of a strange happening in a large Long Island park. Supposedly, an unidentified flying object had landed deep in the woods. Randy heard this "story". He did not know if it was true or not. He did know of some people who observed large military trucks hauling pieces of metal from the park, to an undisclosed place – off Long Island [area 51?]. He didn't believe much of the information from the "fake local news channels". Sadly, those news reporters were a group of dipshits, with limited understanding of truth. In fact, he was convinced that the daily hate spewed from these dogs [as well as dog supporters] got to such a level...

that they really "believed their own lies". He tried to rationalize it. It really was simple. Either "A", most people could not deal with reality, so they created lies to buffer their minds from true horror. Or "B", they were simply dipshits, pure evil – which was very possible and more likely the case.

In any event, Ivanka and Randy enjoyed "exploring". So, weather the UFO story was bullshit or not… it was a cool day trip to the large park to explore! They made the day trip as exciting as possible. Ivanka brought her back pack with a compass, flash lights, etc. She also packed a nice lunch, and they had a picnic in the middle of the park. A nice natural river flowed through the park. And, on a large rock they ate their lunch, together… they did not find any odd alien objects…

The End (continued in chapter 3)

THE ADIRONDACK ADVENTURE

CHAPTER 3

The winter session went by fast, too fast. Ivanka and Randy enjoyed all the time together. They found efficient ways to explore local beaches, share lunches [picnics] and squeezed in time with friends and family. It was now the spring semester. They were situated on campus and ready to dive into another cycle of academic studies. They implemented the same scheduling approach as prior semesters. Always keeping one day to sleep late, together. After all, they knew they would be challenged with many other late nights and extensive blocks of time apart – as they worked diligently through the curriculum. It's not like they were complete animals. They deserved a late morning together – only true lovers would understand that. Just prior to the start of each semester, a trip to the University book store was needed. In the store, at this time in life, was the need to purchase "paper copies of text books". Lots of text books. For a typical science major, enrolled in four courses, the textbook costs ranged between $700 and $1,400 – each semester. This included lab supplies, like dissecting kits and laboratory manuals. There was something about a "fresh" [new or used version] crisp textbook. Perhaps, it was just the start of a new exploration into the literature? Or perhaps it was just an affinity to acquire knowledge, which would one day be added to wisdom...

Randy and Ivanka found themselves in an afternoon ecology lab. In fact, the lab literally took place in a large University "greenhouse". It was nice to get out of the cold and learn about tropical plants, indigenous local plant life and the survival techniques [more like the evolutionary traits] of lizards! They sat together in a small sized class [20 students]. This was not the typical University class size. But, they were half way through their program = Official "Juniors" at the University. The design of the college curriculum started with large class sizes (800+), and decreased significantly by the time one reached the second to third year of studies. There had been a few reasons for this. Some students went into different areas of science. For example, they may have changed their focus to "chemistry".

Others changed their focus to more "physics" curriculum. Ivanka and Randy continued on the path to learn more of the "biological sciences". Evolutionary plant growth and lizard survival was smack in the middle of the curriculum! Ivanka had her long-term sights on entering a medical school program. Randy was thinking about more of an industry setting – in the field of microbiology. In the evenings he thought he may continue with sharing knowledge as an adjunct professor... but that was far into the future... to do that, a master's degree in biological sciences with in-depth experience would be needed. For now, he had enough on his plate – learning the curriculum at the undergraduate level... Randy was daydreaming about Ivanka as they listened to the ecology professor's lecture. She would most certainly make a great medical doctor. She was brilliant, sharp and social. Randy was more of the hard-core research type that found his niche in deep academic studies to differentiate complex concepts… and apply those complex principles to real-life mechanisms…

They were working with lizards that camouflaged into the plant life. This was a particularly good survival approach. And evolutionary traits always favored "survival". You could imagine the wild jungle. There were many different predators. So, one way to protect a lizard's life was to find a plant and hide with it. It was no ordinary plant though. It would need to be a "toxic plant" [one evolutionary technique]. That way, not too many predators ate the plant and the lizard "blended" into the plant by changing its skin colors to mirror the plant. The predator would avoid eating the toxic plant and also would not be able to see the lizard! Other lizards blended into tree branches, changing their skin color to a dark/light brown, etc.

Randy had been having the most vivid dreams at night. He talked to Ivanka about the details of these "visions". He could see some local Long Island towns, where evil thrived. And he realized that these "evil things" [they were not human beings, just bodies with blackened souls or sadly no soul at all] had implemented a similar evolutionary trait, to match the lizard's survival! The evil did not change the color of their skin. No. But, what they did do was somewhat "more clever" and "devious". They changed their social manor to mimic "kindness" and "sympathy" of a nice bright soul. And the evil was extremely good at "playing on its predators". Of course, the predators were the "good souls". This was "psychologically twisted", but very true. Randy spoke of his detailed dreams. He spoke of how these evil entities were so good at this evolutionary trait, that the general public actually felt "sorry for the evil's circumstances". And as the "general public" continued to "feel sorry for the circumstances of this blended evil", the evil force continued to sicken, poison, hurt and destroy lives of good societal people. Even to the point of COLD BLOODED MURDER!

It was something that was difficult to prove, something above the everyday law. More of a Steven Segal approach to combatting the evil. More like a "Cobra Stallone Movie" approach to targeting the incredible "NETWORK" of "EVIL". The evil hid behind the kindness of "family", hid behind the "relationships" of a good society. In fact, the evil went as far as to excommunicate any good soul that threatened their "SECRET". The evil network was thick. It was routed in the local communities. And it also had an important "enabling force". The enabling force were the politicians at the highest state level, and even included some representatives in the HOUSE OF CONGRESS! These elements continually fueled the evil plans: day in and day out, year in and year out, decade in and decade out… etc. The evil had money coming in, the evil had a "sense of eternal security" by these shithead politicians. AND, THE RESULT = were decades upon decades of DESTROYED LIVES. The continual destruction of good souls. However, in the end – weather here on earth or in the afterlife, there would be justice. Similar to the Russel Crowe Gladiator movie scene – where he clearly communicated that there would be justice in "this life" or the "next", to the murderous politician. And Randy believed that, with a heavy heart – with sadness. Because, he never wished destruction on anyone – even on his own enemies.

Some people do not have souls. And others have such blackened souls, that there is no humanity left in them. And those types of evil entities most likely would not even get the chance to spend time in "purgatory". There would be no after life path to the gates of heaven. Sadly, these evil "people" would – in fact – go straight to HELL. Randy did not know how he knew that. He just knew that. It was a gift, a glimpse into the "after life". He felt that sometimes this "gift" was more of a curse, that weighed heavy on his heart at times. Not an opinion, just a clear vision of "what had always been", "what was", and "what will always be". A justice outside of the local law. The justice of nature. A justice of divine wisdom. Ivanka noticed Randy's face. He seemed emotional, tearing… he was sad at the "day dreams" he was having. She hugged him. He said "let's get some PAPA JOHN's pizza" – I would love to hear you talk in the private booth of the pizza restaurant [their private place… she smiled at Randy]. The private booth was not only good for some conversation… she wanted to kiss him, she needed to do more than kiss him… class had ended and they were off to get some pizza, together… always together. The stroll across the forest filled campus grounds was romantic. It was peaceful. Some people don't ever take the time to stroll through nature, hand in hand with their love. There is something about the time that "just disappears", while walking through nature. Almost like time and space do not exist. The only thing that exists during that stroll is two people sharing a smile, enjoying the sounds of surrounding birds/insect/squirrels... There were many bike paths to explore the campus. The paths were followed by the bicyclists or people strolling along. Some of the trees on campus held so much history. They were large oak trees. Beautiful pine and birch trees. Some of the trees were "engineered" by researchers to exhibit a nice glow at night. The tree was spliced with the bioluminescence reaction. It was pretty to see, as they strolled along the glowing trees at night. The lights, via tree bioluminescence, also offered a cost-effective approach to electricity!

The private restaurant was empty when they arrived. Randy got the usual – two personal pizzas and coca cola. Ivanka was seated in the corner booth, surrounded with empty tables/chairs and a dim lit environment. It was nice, quiet and serene. They ate dinner and talked about a really challenging chemistry lab quiz. It was a take home quiz. These types of quizzes always seemed to be the most difficult for this inorganic chemistry class. The challenging part were the questions. They consisted of the most complex formulas, requiring multiple process steps where "units" needed to be changed to match other equational "units". And at the end of the "quiz solutions", was a final step to enter the answers into a computer data base. The worst part of this was that if the "units" didn't match perfectly or if the exact number did not match the correct answer, perfectly – it was not accepted into the data base. And if this "technical" number, which took hours to arrive at, was not accepted in the stupid computer program, it was marked as "incorrect". With these science courses at University, it was always a constant struggle to learn the most complicated theories – and apply them to real life problems. Everything counted. The quizzes, only being a percentage of the overall grade, was just as important. Failure to get the maximum credit would adversely impact the final grade. And by the very end of the semester that "final grade", in these challenging courses was typically, was historically a 40 to a 60 percent. That was an "A", with the competition, with the statistics of the student performance. Each student was aware of this and each student knew they needed to get the maximum amount of points on their quizzes to help get them close to an "A". Randy was a solid B student at University. With course grades of C and As. It all averaged to an approximate B level student. That was something to be proud of. First of all, to be proud that he did not flunk out – like the large population of others. Proud that a B was not too bad, with consideration for the major: pre-med, biological sciences (with interest in music and sociology). As for Ivanka: solid A, she was brilliant, and that was something to always admire.

They held hands, and just relaxed as they sipped the coca cola. A small group of students sat in the near distance, eating pizza. They could hear the conversations. It was interesting. The students were senior level, and about to graduate. They were ahead of Ivanka and Randy. One of the students would be graduating with a biology degree, bachelor of science. He was heading to Florida to enter a United States military program. The Navy needed engineer/science types to ride their nuclear-powered submarines. After an intense two year military academic program – this student (Alex) would see the world as a nuclear submarine Officer! Another student at the table was talking about an exam he sat for with the US Navy, in Manhattan [at One PENN Plaza]. The written exam had a large science and math section, which he breezed through with no issues. The questions were similar to University style physics questions, organic chemistry questions and calculus math questions. However, the second part of the exam he failed miserably! Most of the questions were "photos" of an airplane and its relation to the mountain or ocean. The positioning of the jet with its surroundings, positioning, propulsion, etc. The military officer advised that the student could not be a fighter pilot because he would crash the plane into the mountain! He had limits in his "depth perception". The recruiter did offer a school in Florida for a year of attendance... followed with a commission as a US Navy Officer. After the training, the student would spend four years on a surface warfare ship – out at sea. And, within that time he could apply for a two-year graduate school in California. The school would qualify the student to train dolphins. The dolphins helped US Navy operations in various parts of the world. Dolphins are smart! They can sniff out sea mines and be used to help with various military war time operations. And the final student talked happily about marrying after graduation from the University. Ivanka smiled at Randy and grabbed him under the table. Let's take option 3! Marriage! And she followed with a deep kiss, and hug!

In a town not too far from University was a small suburban neighborhood. The town was modest, with small homes - built in the pine woods Of Suffolk County Long Island. Local fire departments and ambulance companies helped the community, around the clock, seven days each week. The ambulance company in Medford was responsible for arriving at "health crisis scenes". The chief of the ambulance company was a stocky, balding man with a large body frame. He enjoyed socializing in the community and ensured that the ambulance company was ready for health crisis... his name was George. And he was a friendly man. Too friendly. He had connections within the community. Many decades of connections with town level politicians and state level politicians. The connections kept the ambulance company finances afloat. The training for young students was good. George was simply "bad". He also had connections with a network of evil. Any "perceived obstacle" to George's psychotic plans would be met with "death". If not death, "accidents". The accidents resulted in the serious hurting of human health. A broken bone, an odd problem with an organ system. Odd medical conditions as a result of "mysterious circumstances". A little bit of poison added to a child's lunch. A sprinkle of poison to a young adult's lunch. A few milliliters of poison to the soda of an elderly enemy of George's. The pattern of deaths, the pattern of "sickness" was never caught. There was a network of "evil" in the town and in other areas. The network protected this plaque of evil.

The major issue with the ill plagued community was two-fold. The first issue was that evil had existed in the community for many generations. Many decades of the evolution occurred, and present day home owners resided deep in the town. The evil had its hooks in local businesses and local school districts. It did not stop there. The evil flowed into local dental offices, and local doctor's offices [for children and adults]. Riding the town ambulance was a good experience for the "good souls". And many good people did also live in the community. George loved that because to him it was a sport. That is to say, a sport in the sense that evil would search for good to "persuade", "to change". And if that did not work, [if George could not infect the good souls of the town with evil] he would simply kill them. Sometimes, the "accidents" did not result in death. George would still smile though, as long as the good soul was "hurt" or "maimed" in the sporty attempted murder.

The community in Suffolk County New York needed to be fueled from above. Evil does not thrive in a vacuum. No, the evil was street savvy. The evil knew that they needed to collaborate. That is where the local suburban women enter. Most women are good, most women are "ladies". However, there was a group of "so-called ladies" that existed in the suburban community. They were infected with "evil" and they worked diligently behind the scenes, with the "agenda". The agenda was simple: thrive in their community, and destroy all that was good.

It was "for sport". These evil entities thrived in "America" by hiding behind all that was good. They hid in "the family unit". They hid "in the volunteer ambulance organization". They hid in the local "school districts". And, if confronted, this evil was extremely savvy in "playing a victim card". This evil knew what to do, knew what to say and were very good at putting on a show! One approach to further support the evil, was to use the "female parts" to continue to spread the evil in the community. The infection was selective, always looking to utilize their parts to infect leaders of the town, leaders of a hospital, leaders of a school system, leaders of a business, etc. It was more than hate. It was more than misery. It had evolved and coexisted with criminals over many decades. It started with simple criminal activity, like steeling US mail. And, over time the simple criminal activity evolved into more complex situations. Evil enjoyed some of the complexity. It was "for sport". The complex situations that criminals in the community looked for was "creating accidents", that had a goal to cause MURDERS.

The community was supported by the finances of the town and by the financial structure of the state. The evil owned houses in the community. And they were well financed. The news stations and news papers were controlled by this evil. It was a network, and it was routinely fueled with events – every day, every week, every month, every year, etc. A perfect network, especially when planning the next attack on a victim. Riding the ambulances in the middle of the night was the most optimal chance to inflict evil in the community. An enemy that needed transport to the local hospital, also needed some "assistance in the ambulance". And that was where some of the accidents would happen. A sprinkle of low-grade poison, this was one way to secure the agenda-just prior to getting the body to the hospital…

Randy and Ivanka completed their semester's work at University. It was already spring time and the weather was changing. The warm pre-summer air felt good, as the breeze moved gently passed them. They were preparing for another summer in the Adirondacks. But first, the students needed to gear up for an intense two weeks of final exams. They were ready for the final exams and thought it would be a good idea to blow off some steam at the Long Island beaches. There were many great beaches on Long Island, and they were familiar with all of them. It was a sunny Saturday morning when they left the campus, together. Ivanka packed a lunch in a cooler – with snacks.

Long Island is just that, a LONG patch of land. And driving out east was always a nice way to spend a day. Driving east, on the island there was a road that went straight out to the very end. This was called the "south fork" of the island. And at the very end was "Montauk point". Just prior to the end of the island was a great beach called "Hither Hills". Ivanka pulled Randy's pick-up truck into the Hither Hills beach. The parking lot was empty. Tourist season would not start until memorial-day weekend [late May would certainly then show a full parking lot].

It was a warm day, a good day to soak up the sun rays. Ivanka and Randy sat on the beach with a portable radio. Ivanka wore a cute bikini and Randy helped her apply sun tan lotion to her soft skin. Ivanka returned the favor. The sea was choppy, with some cresting ocean waves. It was far from a calm day. Randy suspected that just south of Long Island, there was probably a storm. The waves crested and the water appeared this way when storms were approaching. They finished their time on the beach with a slow, peaceful walk along the ocean water. It was nice, and they searched for sea shells as they strolled along, hand in hand. The sun was setting and they took some great photos. The pictures would be added to a memory book, but was not needed because the memories of the photos would live on in each other's minds. Randy picked up the beach blanket and shook the sand off it. Ivanka packed what remained of the picnic lunch. Walking back to the car, they travelled through a deep tunnel. The tunnel connected the main part of the beach with the car parking lot. About halfway into the tunnel, Ivanka noticed a door. What was strange about this door was a luminescent glow that pierced a small space. She stopped at the door, with curiosity....

The door was locked, and they were unable to open it. Randy found a steel bar, located near the walk way. He used it to pry the door open. Once inside, they noticed a stair way that went deep underground. The steps were dimly lit with luminescent light. Ivanka followed Randy, as they slowly moved down five levels of steps. It went pretty deep, and at the final step they viewed a long corridor. They figured that the pathway went in the direction, back toward the beach. And as they walked it, in the dim light – they could feel the coolness of the ocean. The walls leaked with ocean water and a sound of crashing waves were clearly heard above them…. Back in the local Long Island towns, it was community life, as usual. No red flags were ever flown since the "murders" were slyly performed with enough space. There was enough space in time and in place of incidents. The ambulances were the perfect place to commit a murder. A distressed patient that was "black listed" as an enemy of the town was easily targeted. Along the transport between the home of the "enemy community member" and the hospital, the evil worked its magic. And mysteriously, the patient was "DOE" [dead on arrival] at the local hospital.

Ivanka and Randy thought it would be best to retreat back to the University. They needed to collect their thoughts and their plan needed to include a conservative approach. This was a good way to proceed, given the circumstances – there were just too many "unknowns". Why in the world was there a secret passage underneath the Long Island beach. And where did it lead to? Ivanka packed a school bag, and filled it with flash lights. Water bottles and protein bars were also included – they were essentials. Randy added two large, sharp pocket knives. Ivanka would keep her dorm room during this summer session. She needed to complete research on campus. That meant that both Randy and Ivanka would have a place to sleep for the warm quiet months. However, the trip to the Adirondack mountains would be consolidated – and only include short weekend getaways. They were thankful that they would be able to enjoy the nature this summer, even if it was only some extended weekends.

Back at the beach, Randy opened the locked door and they headed down the stairs. Ivanka turned on two flash lights and proceeded to walk the long narrow path – underneath the beach. The walkway opened to a large laboratory. And in the center of the dark room was a lab bench with various sophisticated computer systems. They sat at the work station and started reading the operation manuals. These were instructions to board one of two "trams". The first was "A tram" and the second was "B tram". Ivanka read the instructions gracefully, quickly and processed the technical information. Tram A headed further out into the Atlantic-ocean [following an underground tunnel]. The tunnel snaked deep, under the ocean – then rose to a docking station. The dock was located in some mysterious island – with coordinates southeast of the Montauk Point, Long Island. The second tram, was located far across the lab room – completely opposite the direction of tram A. There were additional boarding instructions for tram B, because it did not head deep into the ocean. The tram B did not head deep through Long Island. Tram B was railed with nano technology and cross-stitched with the strongest material known to earth. And these nano-sized [not able to be seen with the human eyes] tracks were secured with a clear tube. So, within the clear tube lay nano sized tracks – which went straight up. The vessel on the track was big enough for two people to board. Randy asked where it went too? Why would a tram have this orientation? Ivanka did not know. She did not know yet, but she would certainly find the answer to that last question.

Ivanka recalled a University Physics lecture. The professor spoke to the possibility of building a transport straight to the nearest object in space. A space station, the moon, another planet...and so forth. The technology was there. It was just a matter of designing the blue prints and building it! She smiled and suspected that this was something big! Just where it went to, and why it went there was the concerning parts to this mystery...

The End (continued in chapter 4)

THE ADIRONDACK ADVENTURE

CHAPTER 4

Tram A.

The tram station, located deep underground was not so easy to get to. The tunnel that connected the Long Island beach with the car parking lot housed the entry way to the underground bunker. The locked door was pried open by Randy. That was easy enough. It was the subsequent journey down the stairs and through the underground tunnel that was challenging. Thank goodness for Ivanka. There were at least four different tunnel check points. At each check point was a computer console that required a technical password. Ivanka was technically savvy! She cracked each code with ease, and Randy thought that some would certainly get the wrong impression about the situation. It was a challenging situation. It was filled with difficulties. Working side by side with brilliant Ivanka lightened the load. The "impossible" became "possible". In the center of the bunker, where the deepest point of the tunnel was reached – they found a large system. The system controlled: tram A and tram B. Together, they decided to venture into tram A. Ivanka activated the central bunker computer station. The tram A was lit up and ready to go. Randy and Ivanka entered the vehicle. It was a spacious capsule that had plenty of leg room and a place to store supplies. In fact, there were some basic food supplies [canned items and water] found in the capsule. Ivanka closed the capsule door and within less than a minute they were on their way. Where they were headed was the mystery.

The underground tunnel opened into a clear tunnel, as they moved at a moderate speed. The tunnel snaked through the open ocean! They could see the ocean surround the path they were traveling. A small screen was activated and a video played. The video shed some light into the situation they found themselves in! Ivanka and Randy were heading to an island, located some distance from the Long Island beaches. The video was short, but appeared to have been recorded a long time ago… [probably in the early 1900s]. They could tell by the clothes people were wearing and the way they spoke. The trip was bumpy… They arrived at a docking point, on the island. Immediately, they left the small building [more like a small wooden structure housing the capsule] together. Ivanka noticed a change in their environment. The sky looked different. The air seemed very clean and fresh. Even cleaner and fresher than mountain air; if that was possible. There was no sign of human life. Only deep dark forest. Ivanka sensed that they had traveled to another place in time. Specifically, they had traveled back in time. She did not know for sure... it was a woman's intuition. And that was good enough for Randy. They sensed something was wrong here and tried to get back to the capsule. They could not get the capsule to activate. They were trapped! Just outside of the small building Randy found a row boat. One option was to sail the seas to get back to Long Island. They thought it over for a few minutes. Then decided to keep that on the table. First, they wanted to try to see what they could find in the jungle…Panic was not an option. Similar to attacking the most complex problem at University, they first listed all of the givens: what did they have? The givens included a backpack with protein bars and water. They had flash lights. There was a transport capsule that they could not use to get back to Long Island. There was a boat, with roes, that could be used to sail back to Long Island. The island that they were on seemed desolate. The forest looked deep, and there was no sign of human life.

Ivanka took note of the island's fruit and vegetation. One of the first plans they had was to collect food. So, that is what they did. As Ivanka organized the collected island food, Randy explored the island. He found a man-made shed. The shed was filled with supplies, and that was a good thing. Randy and Ivanka explored the storage shed. It was obvious that at one time, there were humans on this island. The interior of the storage shed was packed with survival gear. There were medicines, travel instruments [compasses], clothes, a shower and soap. They were thankful for this shed. In it, was enough for survival. A shelter from the outside. A bed with blankets. Food and additional gear.

The rain fell violently outside the shed. It was evening, dark and cold outside. Inside Ivanka and Randy lay in bed, with a warm blanket – together. There was something romantic about being secluded, while the pitter patter of violent storm water splashed outside. They thought they could hear some howling in the distance, as well. Randy made sure the door was locked and windows were secured. A good night's sleep was their intention. But, how could they sleep well – surrounded with animals. It was okay, things would change – sooner or later. They found things to do, to calm their minds. Ivanka spoke of her suspicions. How was it possible? That the technology to travel here existed…and that no humans were present? Something happened. Something tragic. She sensed that they had in fact traveled back in time. Somehow – through the snake of a tunnel that connected the Long Island beach to this island. She often had visions of what had been, what was – and that was a gift. Or a curse, depending on how one viewed it. Her minor at University was immunology. The study of the microscopic world – the viruses and microbes that lived there. And the coevolution with species of planet earth. Viruses, for example, had been present much longer than bacteria, yeast, mold, animals and humans. Viruses evolved to survive and thrive. They did this by utilizing natural resources. And eventually, by using the cellular mechanisms found in animals and found in the human cell. With the cellular mechanisms [the nucleus, the cell organelles], the virus could effectively replicate and spread. With the ultimate goal of survival.

In evolutionary terms and in pragmatic/real life terms – viruses were here, had been here and will always be here. They were not going anywhere. Something happened. Perhaps a sly mutation in the genetic material. A mutation that changed its ability to be lethal toward its host. And that may have explained the vanishment of all humans here. Ivanka did not want to get paranoid. But she left the bed and went over to the medicine cabinet. She found what she was looking for. Just precautionary measures: we start pumping our bodies full of zinc and other necessary tablets. This will fight off any potential viruses. Randy brought her some rationale calmness. He said: "what ever happened here, happened and it is over", let's just be careful and we will be okay. You know, like being careful when you come back to bed. We are not looking to procreate, at least – not right now. He smirked, followed with a giggle. She jumped into his soft humor, and smiled. As the rain pitter pattered outside, and the animals growled in the distance – Ivanka made love to Randy. She was passionate, she was soft and lady like. And at times she was more aggressive and even more passionate, with a calmed animal like behavior. Randy loved that wholeness of love. They fell asleep together. Tomorrow would be a day of exploration. They wanted to see if there was more to find on the island...

Randy stood up and made his way to the shower. Ivanka quietly followed him into the bathroom. Quiet as a cat on the prowl. Randy smiled, and offered some soap for her bare skin. The water was warm and eventually hot! There must be a hot water heater around here! This shack had all the essentials. A supply of canned food, a shower, running water, hot water, a bed, and survival gear. There must be more! There must. Why would anyone build such a transport and have a shed full of this stuff, if there wasn't more? The connection between the two souls was more than visual. It was felt and could only be "really felt", at that moment. Where the presence of Ivanka and Randy, together received and sent an intense level of signals. Signals of desire, signals of lust, signals of more than just physical attraction – signals of "connection..." and each potent amount of such traits were sent via a biological "pheromone". Amazing, and also mysterious to anyone, everyone – even to the lovers. Words don't accurately describe all of it. It was more of a "feeling", more of a "protective force in nature", an assurance of survival in this life and into the next life [where ever that went to...].

They sported some pretty cool archeological adventure clothes, found in the shed. Not bad! Pretty cool. Not only were they the part to this adventure, but they were also "dressed for the part"! Too many times people dress a part in this life, without completing the essential levels – needed to actually get to the "part". That is to say, for example, to bypass acquiring knowledge. To bypass the fundamental foundation of essential academia. Without this essential foundation, there is a gap. A gap that is extremely difficult to fill, once bypassed [although, not impossible to fill – just extremely difficult to fill...]. Moving through the intense challenges of five to ten year academic programs, a solid foundation needs at least this investment in time. [This investment in partial amounts of suffering, partial amounts of sacrifice... and of course some moments of priceless joy]. Ahead of the foundational investment is "application of this knowledge base", in the real world, with real life challenges... And Randy was happy to follow Ivanka. She did not have the "completed level of academic achievement", but she did have a "junior levels worth", with real life "experience from a former life…". And that was good for Randy – he felt that they made an almost unstoppable team… which was needed in this "uncharted world, uncharted territory".

Okay, we have water, protein bars, flash lights, lighters, and some medicine… they proceeded to further explore the island. This was a strange situation. How in the world could such an organized path and shed exist, with no human life in sight? Walking deep into the woods, located behind the shed – they found a sign! An actual sign, similar to a "rail road" sign. And not to far from that sign, were rails. The train was modest in construction, but had some kind of electrical power source that still worked. So, they boarded the train and headed deeper into the jungle… The train snaked through the jungle, similar to a ride in an amusement park. Although, they did not feel the joy and excitement of a theme park. They traveled moderately fast through the overgrown jungle for a good hour. And then arrived at a central facility. The structure was embedded, deep in the jungle. The entrance was located just opposite where the train had stopped. The interior building was dark, with no natural light and no electricity. Ivanka removed the flashlights from her back pack. They traveled to a circuit breaker and found a way to get the interior power supply on. Who knew what the power source was? For all they knew, it was a small ball of radioactive isotope…Moving forward, in the lit facility they found a weapons grade governmental research laboratory. The gowning airlock was the largest space Randy had ever seen. Typical gowning airlocks could only fit one person at a time. And while in the airlock, the scientist would carefully strip to the bare essentials…then enter a full body suit. The suit protected the skin from biological agents. This gowning airlock could fit at least five scientists! What an incredible research operation! Ivanka and Randy ensured that each suit was secured. The last part of the procedure they found was to place a helmet on [which covered their entire head to neck region], with a special filtration system. As they entered the large, main part of the lab – they wore a full body suit, latex gloves, feet coverings, and a self-ventilated helmet – with microphone.

Let's see what they have been up to, shall we? Ivanka smiled - you really are a super nerd, aren't you - Randy? They laughed... They were both excited. They needed to find out what had really happened on this island. Immediately, Randy entered the walk-in freezer. There it is! A supply of frozen research viruses. These babies could stay frozen for ever... [like the eradication of the small pox virus??? Wasn't there two frozen stock piles of the small pox virus in US Georgia and in Russia???, just in case???]. What were they researching? Ivanka entered a walk-in incubator that housed a large supply of eggs! This was it. They were growing viruses! Ivanka and Randy met in the center of the lab, at a work station. They sat and looked curiously shaken. That's it. That is all ya need. A supply of eggs and some super viruses. Combine them, and you are growing large supplies of viruses. Randy found a rabies virus, an influenza virus and additional labeled strains…

It seemed that they were weaponizing these viruses! A perfect weapon of CBR – chemical, biological and radiological warfare. The best biological agent would be one that could target so many people… target them, infect them and incubate; undetected for one to two weeks… until it was too late. By the time the virus was detected in the population, the growth already would occur, exponentially. There would be no stopping it. Only natural selection and some savvy experts could tackle this SOB (son of a bitch). Randy proposed that they get the hell out of there, take a long shower… and regroup… Ivanka and Randy quickly left; after taking some of the top-secret protocols with them! They planned to stay one additional night, on the island. They wanted to read through the technical protocols, to get a better understanding of what may have happened. Virology was a fascinating subject. Ivanka and Randy both enrolled in a virology course at University. It was part of the biological sciences college curriculum. The professor, Dr. Lipson was an expert in the field. He taught science at University and performed various research projects at a large government laboratory: Brookhaven National Labs, Long Island New York. The viruses on earth had been here for a long time; he would start his lectures with. A longer time than even bacteria, yeast, mold, animals and humans! Randy wasn't a plant expert, but wondered the evolutionary lineage of viruses and plant life on earth. It was clear that these protocols had been written to investigate novel viruses, from a broad spectrum of viral families. Everything from the common cold [adeno virus] to bio safety level 5 stuff [Ebola virus]. Level 5, where complete gowns, helmets/face masks, filtered air was required as a safety measure – during virus experimentation. In the natural environment, the typical virus and even the atypical [mutated form] virus traveled across the globe – with the seasons. What was actually happening, though, was that the virus coevolved with "natural hosts". In the natural host, they did not cause illness. They were just there in a sort of symbiotic or more likely non-symbiotic relationship. It was a good evolutionary mechanism for survival of the viruses… As birds migrated across the globe, for instance…

the viruses travelled with them. Dr. Lipson would make interesting technical lecture points about the industrial revolution. The fact that the building and development into deep forests, where no one had ever been – was sometimes problematic. A novel virus would "appear" after some industrial development...and would quickly spread via people traveling across the globe, on planes. Most viruses had a natural host in the animal kingdom. There were also other natural "reservoirs". Like the HIV-1 and HIV-2 viruses, with original reservoirs in the African monkey [mangobey, if Randy recalled correctly]. It was not a good evolutionary approach to "completely wipe out"/ "destroy" a host though. Then the virus would have no place to infect. So, the natural transmission of viral infection typically followed nature's growth curve. Initial infection [into a host's cell], followed by dormancy for one to two weeks [depending on the strain], an explosive replication phase – where exponential growth was observed and much destruction occurred, followed by a plateau for some time and eventual decline [as hosts were reduced, nutrients were diminished and environmental shifts happened].

The concern that Ivanka had was not with the typical viral progression. Something else happened on this island. A serious, nonnatural mutation. A bioterrorist agent experiment that went wrong, and exploded into the air! The mutation was new and not natural, infecting at a massive rate – with utter, total destruction of its host. The host was humans! They read enough of the technical literature to get a good night's sleep. What ever happened was over. But, where had all the people disappeared to? The howling in the night sky troubled their thoughts. Could it be possible that the infection mutated these people into some sort of beast? They were not going to stick around long enough to find out. The next morning, they gave the tram A one additional go. It did not work. So, they boarded the row boat and referenced some maps found in the shed. According to the maps, the distance to Long Island shores was within reason – they could do it. With water, compass, flash lights, maps and some protein bars – they began to paddle in the ocean water, leaving the island behind.

The row boat handled well in the open ocean. It was a nice sail boat, without sails though! Randy offered to start with the rowing. They talked during the peaceful journey.

Ivanka calculated the distance from the shed map, with a formula. She estimated that the boat ride would take four to six hours. They continued their discussion about the findings of the island. Ivanka smiled at Randy; "sometimes, knowing too much could cause paranoia!" He smiled, laughed and agreed. She continued... recall that the plague was pretty bad, and it killed many... the "black plague". And what caused it? Not a government experiment that went bad... no, it was simply from the natural environment. The black plague was caused by a BACTERIA! "yersinia pestis", which is commonly found in natural reservoirs of prairie dogs... and other natural ecosystems... and look what that bacteria caused... Ivanka's point was that they needed to gather more information, before concluding that the "missing island people" was a result of a bad virus experiment. The wind was with them, the tide was heading toward Long Island… they would be there shortly… Randy took a few breaks to share a drink of water and share protein bars, from Ivanka's back pack…

Long Island - the desert

The sailing was not that bad, even though there was a lack of "sails". The ocean current was with them, and there was a nice breeze the whole way toward Long Island. The compass had worked well, and thebearings navigated the boat to Patchogue harbor. From there, they started to walk. It was not long before they noticed that something was very odd. It was Long Island, with some buildings… but the structures were of "initial phases", just beginning to be built. There was not one soul walking through the towns. The cars that they did see, were not of this time. It was the early model Ts, Ford! To see this was interesting… to not see any people, well - that was disturbing. Randy managed to get one of the cars started and they made their way to the University. It was a twenty to thirty-minute drive north of Patchogue, along roads that were not familiar. At the University it was clear that construction was basic… initial phases of buildings. Many campus buildings were missing and the landscape had changed.

So much for logic and "paranoia". This was more than an "adventure". This was not exactly "science fiction", and it was not exactly "super-natural". It seemed that it was a combination of the three! If that were even possible… They walked around the strange University campus.

Not a soul was seen… something had happened on that island and it stretched back across the globe… they theorized. What was more fascinating, though, was that when they travelled through the Tram A tunnel, they did not only reach a distant island… no, they also reached another time [sort of a time travel]. They sat and tried to relax their thoughts… Ivanka being the young savvy scientist immediately proposed that they get back to the island… and somehow get back through the tram A tunnel. It was getting late and they needed to rest first… so they found shelter in a dormitory… They planned to get a good night's sleep, collect their thoughts and do some exploring of the Long Island… over a few days or so… Perhaps they would find some humans, some animals. They needed to find some food to eat, more water to drink… and a change of clean clothes….

It was an early morning, with lots of sunlight and a cool refreshing breeze. Ivanka and Randy woke, showered and got ready to explore Long Island. They walked across campus and found their model T car. After placing the backpack, with supplies into the car – they headed out to travel to the northern most part of Long Island. From the Stony Brook area they drove north, following unfamiliar roads. And when they could travel not further, they knew that they would arrive in a town called "Port Jefferson". The landscape was completely different from what they had remembered. There were more farms. There were less buildings. And as they traveled north, following the compass and intuition, they arrived in "Port Jefferson". It was a nice modest town, right on the water – the Long Island Sound. A ferry traveled daily between this town and the northern most land mass, Connecticut.

There were less buildings and the town looked very different. But, the town was there and as they drove the model t ford car deeper into the town, the road descended and moved closer to the ocean. Just before reaching the ferry, Randy parked the car. They walked through the town and enjoyed the time. There were no people and this was strange. Right on the water they found a place, "Danfords". It was a small hotel with a bar-grill. Inside the building they located the kitchen. The kitchen walk-in freezer had plenty of seafood. Randy loved to cook…. The dinner was good, they enjoyed the fresh seafood. Ivanka was wondering where in the world every human being had disappeared to? They decided to leave Danford's, and walk through the town in the night. As they walked, they noticed that their surroundings were unusually quiet. Too quiet. Behind the stores was a small park. They walked into the park and climbed to the top of an iron structure.

The structure was in the shape of a rocket ship. The top platform gave a good view of the town. In the distance, Ivanka noticed a small child walking toward the park. The child was not walking normally, but rather walked with a noticeable dragging of one leg. It was a dark and breezy night. Randy and Ivanka descended from the iron structure, and approached the child. The child was about four feet tall, with a tiny build. As they got closer, they could see that something was not right. This child had been changed. A different type of child stood within arms-length of Ivanka, when sharp teeth gripped into her flesh. Ivanka screamed! Randy grabbed the "child", but was fiercely bitten – multiple times. The child ran off into the night landscape.

Randy asked if Ivanka was okay? She was…but they needed to get back to "Danfords" to clean their wounds. Randy asked Ivanka if she had any of the "cave water", in her backpack. They drank some of the water...and were quickly healed.... The virus must have mutated after entering its host – after entering the human body. Viruses enter the human cell, and use the nucleus to manufacture cellular components. The components are specifically found in the virus' blueprint for life. This blueprint has instructions for virus survival. Basically, the virus "grows" and "grows", then spreads throughout the natural environment – infecting anyone or anything in its path. Ivanka proposed that they head back to eastern long island, where they originally entered the tram, deep in the beach tunnel...They planned to leave in the morning. They did not sleep as well, thinking about the monster of a child that bit them.

What had happened to the community on Long Island? How far had this evil spread? Was it global? Local infection is one thing... but, when the infection is across the globe... then that is a PANDEMIC! The morning sun and ocean breeze woke Ivanka. Her and Randy repacked for the trip out to eastern Long Island. Before leaving port Jefferson, they entered a candy shop. Glucose would be a good snack for the trip. The candy shop had an incredible selection of packaged sugar! Various chocolates, fudge, truffles, bubble gum, soda, water and caramel! They took a good amount and started eating the jaw breakers. Randy always enjoyed the different flavored taffy. Cherry, blueberry, peppermint, chocolate, mint, lemon and lime flavors!

The drive was a quiet one. The land seemed so barren. No animals were observed, and this was odd for the beach area. On a typical day, the deer were prevalent on Long Island beaches. Families of deer, grazing the nearby grass. Deer looking for humans to sneak them KFC chicken and other food.

The beach was empty of human life, of animal life. They parked the Ford Model T car in the large desolate beach parking lot. Ivanka brought the candy filled backpack and Randy followed her to the tunnel entrance. Halfway into the tunnel they found the locked door. Randy again pried it open. This time it was different. Someone had been in the tunnel, someone or something had entered/reentered the tunnel ahead of Randy and Ivanka. They proceeded cautiously. With flashlights lit, Ivanka and Randy walked down the stairs into the corridor that housed Tram A and Tram B. In the central console area were two people. A gentleman in his early forties, wearing a white lab coat. He sported a nice pair of glasses and a scruffy light beard. The lady next to him was hugging him – they assumed she was his wife. Ivanka introduced herself to the gentleman. They seemed startled, surprised but happy to see human life in this time/place/dimension [whatever you wanted to call it].

The professor's name was Dr. Alex and his wife's name was Carla. Carla was athletic in appearance, with long dark hair and olive skin. She did not sport any glasses, but did have amazingly pretty brown eyes that pierced anyone's soul – when you stared long enough. Ivanka asked simply: "where are we, when are we, what in the world happened here?" The professor presented all the knowledge he knew of the subject matter. It was a modern Shakespearian tragedy. An experiment with good intention, that went awfully wrong. The technology was incredible and it was being used to advance humanity. An island had been purchased off the coast of Long Island. An underground bunker was built, that housed two trams (Tram A and Tram B). The Tram A utilized the advanced technology to travel to a place where a TOP SECRET EXPERIMENT was to be performed. The subject was "virology", the study of a tiny "thing". A thing that could not be seen with the human eye. Even a simple microscope would have difficulty seeing these things. The virus is even smaller than your friendly neighborly bacteria, yeast and mold! The viruses were being studied as part of CBR defense. Understanding CBR would certainly offer an advantage in the event a world war occurred. There were three components of CBR. The experiment focused on the middle component: biological agents. The other two were called chemical agents and radiological agents (e.g., chemical gases and nuclear warfare). Messing with biological agents is no joke, and could result in complete chaos.

The professor continued on and Randy/Ivanka/&the professor's wife listened carefully – with interest and curiosity. The law of entropy was real and has always been present in life. All things have the tendency to become "disordered". Without proper organization, the entropy law will sooner or later lead to disaster…therefore, playing with viruses is a risky business. Some risk was inherently essential during experimentation, if the virologist wanted to gain insight into pathogenicity (the factors that cause disease in humans and in animals). However, if the virologist was looking to splice the right genetic material, with a goal to enhance the pathogenic nature of the "thing/virus…" well, this approach could lead to the "perfect storm scenario". Especially, if the wrong technical expertise or the professor articulated: "the lack of technical expertise" was present in the facility where the research was being performed.

This is not just science fiction and supernatural stuff. The experiment was performed and the results impacted the world! The virus spread across the globe and within a "five-year" period of time… most humans died slow and agonizing deaths. The animal populations were also affected. What little life remained, dwindled to nothing more than "animal instincts". Little thoughts of the human mind. Just a thirst for flesh, for blood. Ivanka stopped the professor. Yeah, we ran into a flesh-eating child. She took bites of Randy and I!

The ethics, the morale, the values of humanity were insufficient. The experiments were performed because they could be. It was amazing and exciting experiments. The travel in time, to the area 50 – as it was called, was truly unbelievable – but true. And that was it. They were trapped in a place and time, with no escape. Ivanka asked if it were possible to return to the "present day". She advised the professor that they had tried to return back through the tram A tunnel (from the island), but it would not work. He looked troubled and immediately apologized for what had happened. Professor Alex and his wife Carla were working diligently on the problems. Their goal was to get the Tram A to return them to "present day", as well.

To date, they were unsuccessful. So, they were all trapped in this place – in this time. The professor added one glimmer of light though... There was a secluded Indian colony that managed to survive, in the Adirondack mountains. Randy and Ivanka smiled. Ivanka offered to help the Professor in the future (if time even ticked in this place). But, Randy and Ivanka also wanted to know about "tram B". The professor replied with an even greater level of FEAR. He simply said: "if you think Tram A was a perfect storm, you would not be able to comprehend what happened with Tram B". And that was it...

Ivanka thanked the gentleman and his wife, for all the knowledge and wisdom. They would be in touch. And one day, perhaps together the serious consequences of these experiments could be forgiven.

Perhaps a cure to all of this could be found. But, not right now. Ivanka grabbed Randy's hand, squeezed and led him to the next chapter of this adventure. Randy followed Ivanka to the Adirondack mountains, where they decided to live, laugh and love.

Just near the nice Adirondack log cabin, was mystical water – hidden deep in a cave.

The End.

Printed in the United States
by Baker & Taylor Publisher Services